P

Dr CEN

HEART AND SOUL

Before the snow arrives and she becomes trapped for the winter, Flora escapes from the village in which she has grown up. Shame and scandal have marred her good name, so she refuses to live her life there — condemned by the unfair judgement of others. However, Flora finds that fate has placed her destiny in the hands of the mysterious Mr Simkin. Together they brave the treacherous weather in order to fight the treachery of men . . .

Books by Valerie Holmes
in the Linford Romance Library:

THE MASTER OF
MONKTON MANOR
THE KINDLY LIGHT
HANNAH OF HARPHAM HALL
PHOEBE'S CHALLENGE
BETRAYAL OF INNOCENCE
AMELIA'S KNIGHT
OBERON'S CHILD
REBECCA'S REVENGE
THE CAPTAIN'S CREEK
MISS GEORGINA'S CURE
CALEB'S FAITH
THE SEABRIGHT SHADOWS
A STRANGER'S LOVE

VALERIE HOLMES

◆

HEART & SOUL

Complete and Unabridged

LINFORD
Leicester

First published in Great Britain in 2008

First Linford Edition
published 2008

British Library CIP Data

Holmes, Valerie
  Heart and Soul.—Large print ed.—
Linford romance library
  1. Love stories
  2. Large type books
  I. Title
  823.9'2 [F]

ISBN 978–1–84782–375–5

Published by
F. A. Thorpe (Publishing)
Anstey, Leicestershire

Set by Words & Graphics Ltd.
Anstey, Leicestershire
Printed and bound in Great Britain by
T. J. International Ltd., Padstow, Cornwall

This book is printed on acid-free paper

1

Ivy, the baker in the village, was busy with her bread when Flora appeared at her back doorway. The village had not fully risen as this was an early hour.

'Oh, lass, it grieves me that it has come to this.' She wiped her hands on her apron and hugged Flora tightly.

'I don't think I woke anyone, Ivy, but I'm scared they'll catch me before I'm safe away.' Flora hugged Ivy back. She was closer to this woman than her own ma, or to be precise, step-ma.

'Look, Flora, you set your sights on that moor road and you climb that bank before the coach comes and don't think about anything other than that. But lass, the weather's changing. There'll be bad storms here soon. Snow and lots of it, heavy and it will stay for days.'

Flora and Ivy had been close confidants for years. However, her friend had speeded up her leaving by telling her she must go before the climate changed for the worse or she would be snowed in. Then she would be trapped like a wild animal in a cage. Perhaps that would be fitting, Flora thought, as she had been looked upon as such a spectacle in recent days.

Ivy was usually correct in her weather predictions, claiming that a soul only had to understand the way that the animals and plants around you acted. The finality — the grief she felt, tore at Flora's heart.

'Look, I've put together some bread and cake for you.' Ivy held out a cloth bundle, lovingly and carefully knotted on the top. 'Now no more messin' about or you'll miss that coach, and lass you must catch that one or you'll be lost.'

Flora took the parcel from Ivy, and, as the woman released her hold on it, Flora's eyes moistened.

'Now stop that, lass. Yer made of stronger stuff and well yer know it. Put that in yer bag and go before everyone's up and they hunt yer down like a witch of old. You go now.' She put her fingers to Flora's lips before she could speak a final few words. 'No need to say anythin', lass. I know what you were thinking, goin' to say as I feel the same. Just go and God's blessin's be upon you. If you make it to Ebton, stay with Sally Riggs and in the spring I'll visit. Now go whilst you still can.'

Flora picked up her bag and skirted around the back of the cottage. She almost ran along the side of the road that climbed steeply from the valley to the open moor. Remembering Ivy's advice, she kept her mind focussed on that one target.

Old Seth was leaving the village on his horse and cart. He was making his way to Groombeck Manor to start his day's work, but he did not see her as he was going up the road to the south moor on the opposite bank; strange, but lucky for her that he had not taken his usual route.

She did not look back at the village, shame-faced, but stared defiantly at the road ahead lettin' both her past and Seth disappear out of sight. She could hardly believe he was the same Seth who had given her rides in that same cart as a child.

Finally she reached the even ground at the top of the bank, and the bracing chill gripped her slender body. Flora steadied herself and looked back down into the vale from where she had just come.

The steep bank had taken her nearly an hour to climb up, dragging her bag with her few worldly belongings inside it. No one would have offered to give her a ride to the top of the steep gradient, such was the depth of her disgrace. She had been spurned by her own kind — made an outcast to the society she had been a part of for the past twenty years, and why? Because she had dared to think of herself in a life beyond her born station; to dare to dream of a life away from everything she had ever known and to love a man from a different place, or at least that was what she presumed was the reason to be.

Her reputation now lay in ruins, as she was thought of as a creature of low or no morals. So they had judged her and so she was supposed to accept a life of scorn and become humble, working off her mistake for the rest of her life. Her lover, in whom she had put her faith and future, was no more, killed in the war, never to return and fulfil those dreams that she had held so dear to her.

Only Ivy saw her genuine pain. Others thought her to be little better than a parasite and her punishment was to live a life where she was only seen fit to marry the lowest worker or oldest man in the village. No eligible male of standing would want to touch her, or so she had been told repeatedly by her mother, or as Flora frequently reminded the woman, her stepmother.

Flora looked at the bag placed upon the frosty ground by her feet. She hitched herself on to her tiptoes, until she could rest her weight on the milestone placed at the edge of the moor road, and then Flora shivered. The vast open expanses offered her little protection against the bitter north-easterly wind that was blowing directly across them.

She waited patiently hugging herself tightly, as the only coat she possessed was ill befitting to protect her against the dropping temperatures. It was made of well worn wool cloth and fitted her slender waist neatly before hanging straight to her feet. It fit her so long as she didn't put on any more weight.

However, she did not see the likelihood of that as, of late, she was permanently hungry. One poor meal a day was simply not enough to keep a person strong, and her 'ma' had told her she did not deserve more. Food was scarce for all, but hers was said to be feeding her will of defiance and the woman had taken advice from the village elders to take action to break her spirit and therefore purge her of her sins.

Flora had suffered too many days of this sentence whilst Ivy had smuggled her the odd victual and made arrangements for her escape.

Flora tried to cheer herself up by thinking about the fresh bread that was lovingly wrapped within her bag. She wanted to eat it there and then, but decided it would be better to wait until she was safely on her way. Then she imagined the coach that would soon be stopping here, as it always did. The locals relied on it and the mail coaches that passed at the same times on the same days, each driver priding himself on never being late.

She stared at the darkening sky. Flora looked up at the bands of uniform grey clouds that were closing in, covering the clear blue that had been there earlier in the day. Ivy must be right about the snow, she thought to herself fondly. She breathed deeply, with a heavy heart, but she was not going to give in to their demands. Flora was going to live a life of her own choice — so long as she had the freedom to make that choice for herself.

The coach appeared in the distance, its high form moving towards her at a pace. She was filled with strange feelings. Fear gripped her and yet another liberating surge of emotions rose within her as she heard the horses' hooves, the rhythmical noise ever louder as they came closer.

Her stomach felt as though it was tying itself in knots. Once she was on this vehicle she knew she could never go back to the village and would have to wait for the spring before she saw her friend, Ivy, once more. One last glance down the vale made her eyes water. In the distance she thought she heard her name called out loud but then the word drifted off into the wind.

The coach stopped not ten paces from where she was standing. She felt the purse in her pocket and the coins that Ivy had given her along with

Martin's final gift to her, and held it firmly — it was her future. It seemed so much to her now, but she did not know how long it would take her to make more money of her own, or how much living would cost beyond the only place she really knew, her own village.

'Good,' she said determinedly to herself, as the driver dismounted. 'It shall be enough. I shall make it so!'

The driver stepped down and picked up her bag. He looked around her as if searching for someone else. 'You travelin' alone, miss?' he asked in his gruff voice, his surprise was clearly audible.

'Yes, I am,' she hesitated for a moment then added, 'Due to a family bereavement, I'm afraid it is — necessary.' She looked down at her feet for a moment to add sincerity and effect to her words. Also to hide her eyes, lest they betray her lie.

'Oh dear, lass, shame that. You best climb in before those storm clouds break, then we can be on our way.' His rough face broke into a smile and he winked at her as he lifted her bag on to the coach. 'Yer can afford the fare for inside, eh? You'll freeze for sure on top in a coat like that.'

'Yes, of course.' She produced her purse and counted out the coins for him. He pocketed it without checking the amount and opened the door for her before climbing back up to his position.

'Harlot! Wench! No one shall touch you again lest they pay first! You're a wanton woman!' The shrill voice echoed from the valley road as a woman emerged at the top of the bank, dishevelled in appearance and breathless after her climb. 'You come back 'ere and face yer shame! Yer pa should have given yer a good beatin' long since!'

'What's that you're sayin', woman?' The driver leaned back down as Flora climbed up into the coach. She deliberately did not look at the passengers sitting inside, but she chose to seat herself quickly and slammed the door shut behind her. She stared anxiously out of the window, watching outside in horror as the woman approached them, arms flailing wildly as her curses continued. Flora was willing the coach to move on swiftly.

She grabbed the leather strap and pulled down the window. 'Driver, go quickly! Please, ignore her, she is out of her mind,' Flora shouted up at the driver, then added, 'They call her Mad Maude — pay her no heed, she rants and raves like that all of the time. Please pay her no mind. She is soon to be placed in the asylum.' Flora slammed the window shut as the driver released the brake. She breathed a sigh of relief as the coach sped into action and her journey into a new life began.

The woman stared at them, shaking her fist aggressively as the coach pulled away. She looked every inch a person possessed as they and Flora travelled out of her reach. Flora subdued the urge to cry as she watched the woman she had been told by her father to call

'Ma' disappear from her vision and her life forever.

The inside of the coach was dark by comparison to the bright grey daylight outside. Flora became aware that a figure, a man, sat on the opposite seat staring out of his window. He was both handsome and looked strong. Next to him, was a boy nervously shrinking back against the seat. It was difficult to judge how old he was — possibly fourteen, she guessed. However, he was slightly built. Like the gentleman, he was quite well dressed in serviceable travelling clothes.

She did not mean to stare at him, or at the man but, as she studied the cape coat he wore and his soldier's boots — fine black and sturdy, he turned his head towards her and Flora found herself looking straight into his dark eyes. As the light caught the side of his face, she could see that he had a faint scar that ran down from his chin to his neck.

It had healed but the skin had the

faint tell-tale mark left upon it, a blemish on an otherwise fine and proud face.

'Ma'am do you wish to ask me something or do you imagine we have met before?' His words were polite, but his manner was brusque — angry even.

Flora was taken aback by his question; however, she had no time for feeling unequal or humble. The last week of her life had been a living hell to her and no one was going to intimidate her in such a way again. She was starting her new life, her very own, on her own terms.

Flora looked him straight in his eyes as her vision adapted to the light, and confidently she politely replied, 'Why, no, sir. I was merely adjusting my eyes to the darkness of the carriage. I did not mean to stare rudely at you . . . sir.' She glanced at the boy, but his eyes would not meet hers. He looked at his own feet instead.

She turned away from him and gazed out of her window towards the open moor. There was an unusual brightness to the day, almost an eerie pure white glow that cast dark shadows over the moors.

'Did my ears deceive me or was the 'irate lady' referring to you in a highly derogatory manner, ma'am?' The man's voice disclosed his open sarcasm.

Flora was furious at his ill manner. He was openly mocking her, and in front of his hapless youth. She held her head high and stared back at him defiantly. 'The woman is quite mad, sir. Whatever it was that she said, I would advise you not to pay it any attention at all! There is no need to repeat the insults of an infirm mind, sir.'

'Good, I would hate to share a carriage with a common 'harlot'. It would ill befit my reputation. I should never feel safe again.' The smirk that crossed his face broadened into a wide grin.

She folded her arms in front of her and felt her cheeks colouring deeply. The boy quickly glanced at her and she thought she saw a flicker of a grin on his nervous face.

'I am not sure what the woman's ravings contained, I was too busy settling myself on the coach and wishing they would do something to restrain her antics. However, can I respectfully suggest, though, that you practice being a gentleman?' Flora looked directly at him, confronting his arrogance head on.

He surprised her by laughing openly and shaking his head. 'Forgive me, young lady. I tease you mercilessly to abate my own boredom. I mean you no insult. You are not like any harlot I have ever seen or met.'

Flora found herself both admiring and resenting his confidence and manner. 'I take it both as a compliment and an apology, as you have perhaps seen and met 'many' in your life and I have not had the pleasure of meeting one.' Flora kept her voice calm and her hands rested gently on her lap.

'Touché!' he returned, then stared out of his window again and for some minutes all was silent, except for the noise of the coach as it travelled along the road at some speed.

Then, as if they had not spoken previously, he removed his hat and said to her, 'You must forgive my manners, ma'am. I have failed to introduce myself to you formally, or my . . . ward. I am Mr James Richmond Simkin and this young man is Frederick, at your service.'

Flora looked at him, slightly taken aback by his sudden polite and proper manner. It was in stark contrast to his earlier outburst.

'I am pleased to be of your acquaintance.' She paused for a moment as if expecting him to laugh at her again as she was not used to making small-talk with gentlemen.

The boy looked up momentarily and smiled at her. Flora smiled back at him, but then she realised that the shadow she thought that was cast on the boy's cheek was actually a bruise. He had been keeping his head low out of shame, as if to hide it. Frederick must have realised that she had seen it and instantly looked downwards again. Flora wondered if this unpredictable guardian or master was the perpetrator of it.

She knew he was waiting for her to answer his introduction in kind and so she forced herself to address him.

'My name is Jessica Mather,' she lied convincingly, impressing herself. However, did starting a new life mean that she had to somehow detach herself from her past, and the mess that lay behind her in the dale. What better way to do it, than to have a new name with which to start a new life?

'Well, Miss Mather, I am most sincere in my previous apology and would wish that we could spend the rest of our journey together in a less tense atmosphere. I take it that you are travelling on your own due to an adverse circumstance.' His manner was much more relaxed and he appeared to be showing a genuine interest in her, but Flora was wary of him. He changed moods like the weather, the moor or the sea.

Flora looked at him and replied solemnly, 'Yes, you heard my words correctly when I spoke to the driver. I am recently bereaved and am travelling to visit my extended family.' Lies were rolling off her tongue so easily that it almost scared her. Was she becoming her own person or a new and dangerous liar? Was she saving her own life or selling her soul to the devil? Flora had no idea, but she had spoken the lies and would have to make good on them.

'It is just that you are not wearing the usual mourning clothes. I admit that I did not take your comments seriously.' There was a note in his voice that she sensed did not sound quite taken in by what she had just said. He had eyes that noticed detail and a mind that was as quick as his sharp tongue. This gentleman, Flora realised, was nobody's fool and therefore could be very dangerous.

'I have had no time to organise such things, sir, nor the money to waste on the usual attire. I need to be more practical in life, sir, with both my time and my money, but my departure from your usual protocol and standards I am sure will be of no concern to you, I am quite certain.'

'Are you?' He raised a brow. 'Well, it isn't. That is, other than over and above my natural concern for my fellow man . . . or woman.' He half-smiled at her.

'Do you always judge people so quickly, Mr Simkin?' Flora asked him, and he answered without hesitation.

'Yes, I'm afraid that I do, miss. You see it is — how can I explain? It's an occupational hazard.'

'And what profession would that be?'

'Look, miss, it's snowing.' Frederick's sudden exclamation surprised them both as he viewed the falling flakes with enthusiasm.

Flora looked out also in wonder as the large flakes fluttered down from the sky. Indeed, it was a heavy storm and

19

the snow was quickly starting to lie upon the ground. Now the shadows were starting to disappear under a white blanket and with each flake her excitement grew. This was her new beginning — a fresh covering over the old shadows of her life. She suddenly felt uneasy, aware that she was being watched, and turned back to the stranger who was openly observing her, studying her in a very attentive and personal way.

'I make no apology, ma'am, for looking at you so. For I see in your face something I have not felt myself for many years.' He smiled, but seemed ill at ease and shifted on his seat.

'You speak in riddles, sir,' Flora replied. 'I'm merely enjoying watching something that I have not seen much of before. It is both exciting and new to me.'

'Then there are many things in this world you have not yet seen. I envy you,' he replied sincerely, yet still appeared to be lost in his own thoughts.

'Then perhaps, sir, it is I who should envy you, if you have witnessed so much in your lifetime,' she answered thoughtfully not completely sure if the man was bragging or not.

'No, never do that.' He settled back on his seat, folding his arms across his broad chest, before closing his eyes.

Flora watched him for a few minutes, expecting him to speak further, but then as he seemed to have settled into a slumber, she returned to watching the snow with Frederick, amazed at how soon it was covering the ground and how old his young face appeared in the light. He too, she thought, had seen more in his short life than her and, as she thought of Mr Simkin, she wondered at whose hands.

She shivered, but it was not with the dropping temperature, but because she realised that escaping her shame was only the beginning. Surviving on her own was not going to be as straightforward as she had thought.

The journey continued in silence as

each tried to settle as comfortably as they could into their own narrow space. The temperature continued to drop as the snowstorm grew in ferocity and then the coach stopped.

'Damnation!' James Simkin exclaimed as he saw how heavy the snow lay outside.

The driver appeared at the door, wind-blown and covered by the drifting snow. He opened the door to speak to Mr Simkin directly. 'It's no good, sir. I can't take the coast road. You'll have to ride it from here. I'll be lucky to make the inn on the Newcastle road before I have to ride on with the mail and abandon the coach. You'd make better way on your horse if you go now, whilst you can still see the road that is.'

Simkin considered the man's words for a moment.

'I don't want to go to Newcastle,' Flora said. 'I need to go to Ebton!' Flora tried unsuccessfully to suppress the panic that she felt rising within her. She knew she had a friend at Ebton, the girl Sally Riggs, who Ivy was related to, and who had married and left their village. She would help her find a position.

Sally, she remembered, was full of fun and always welcomed a challenge. But if Flora went to Newcastle she would be lost. She would not know anyone and that was a dangerous position to be in for a young woman of little means in a large city.

'Then you will have to go with Mr Simkin, ma'am. For the road would be impassable for my coach and horses on a night like this,' the driver explained, but the man Simkin jumped down from the coach and fastened his greatcoat which made him look even more like a military man in Flora's eyes.

'Frederick, stay with the lady.' The man gave orders as if it was his right. 'Miss, go with the coach and Frederick to the inn. I shall return with transport that will traverse the road in the morning.' He tossed a coin purse to the boy. 'Make sure you are both well lodged.' Simkin looked at the driver who nodded in agreement. 'Keep the luggage with you and safe, boy.'

Frederick nodded.

'Don't I have any say in these arrangements?' Flora asked, amazed at the man's arrogance.

'No!' came his short reply as he slammed the coach door shut and told the driver to drive on. Flora opened it and stepped out. She knew that the snow would be too heavy for him to return in the morning. 'Throw down my bag, sir!' she demanded and the driver did.

Mr Simkin could only watch as the coach driver took his vehicle on to safety, leaving her standing at the roadside shivering. Mr Simkin's figure rode towards her on his horse. 'Have you lost your mind, girl?'

'I have to get to Ebton. The snow will be too heavy the morrow — and you know it!' She was cold, furious and scared.

He leaned over and grabbed her arm. 'Come! Climb up here before we both freeze to death, and do not disobey me again!'

2

They rode against the driving snow for a good half hour, the horse slowing as time passed and obviously feeling tired as it fought its way through the storm. It was not possible for Flora to turn and speak to Mr Simkin. All she could do was shamelessly huddle herself as closely as possible in to his body, partially sheltered by the sides of his greatcoat as he had tried to wrap it around her. It was becoming apparent to her that soon they would have to seek shelter from the freezing wind.

Flora brushed away a snowflake that caught on her eyelash and, for one fleeting moment, thought she had seen an illusion. Was the strange light playing tricks on her eyes? She hoped not. Eagerly she pointed ahead of them — a church spire was profiled against the sky's impending gloom by a silvery light. The horse's struggling hooves were directed towards the building's shadowy form.

Flora briefly made out the word from Mr Simkin, it was 'church'. She was seeing correctly and her spirits lifted a little. Relieved, she nestled herself against his body again, feeling the buttons from what she could only presume was a uniform, as the horse stumbled on the frozen ground causing their two bodies to bump against each other at force.

He put a protective arm around her as the horse recovered its footing. Snow drove pitilessly at their faces. The horse was breathing hard. Flora could hear his words of encouragement to the animal, willing it on. Whether it could hear or not, it responded to its master as though it understood the muffled tones; driven by its own determined strength and natural need to survive it brought them to the shelter of the side of the old church.

Against the cold stone wall, they

dismounted and huddled from the relentless fall of the snow. As Mr Simkin took the horse's reins and moved away from Flora to peer around the building she started to shiver uncontrollably. With the body heat of both man and horse removed from her she felt the full force of the cutting temperatures. She was wet from the snowfall, and for the first time since leaving Ivy and the warmth of her bakery with the constant smell of freshly baked bread, she had to admit she was both home-sick and frightened.

She turned the large ring handle on the church door but did not know what to do once she found it was bolted shut. An uncontrollable urge filled her — to cry; the thought disgusted her. She was not weak, and never had been in mind, spirit or body, but then she had never felt so cold in her life before.

Mr Simkin, however, had. He knew exactly what to do. 'Hold the reins, don't let go of them at any cost.' He patted the animal's neck and held them out to her, and this time she willingly obeyed him. The horse was nervous, but she soothed its mane as Simkin lifted up his collar and leaned into the wind, almost limping as he struggled, disappearing from view around the side of the building.

Flora looked at the horse. It twitched and shivered too. She was standing close to the animal as it gave off its own body's warmth. There was something comforting about not being left alone. Behind her there was a grating sound of wood dragging against wood, and the old oak door was opened wide.

'Come in; don't stand out there like a statue,' Simkin ordered, but Flora hesitated.

'The horse will freeze if we leave it here.' She held tightly to the reins, and was surprised when he abruptly took them from her and almost pushed her through the arched doorway, leading the horse inside the church. Flora looked relieved but more than a little surprised by his action. It was what she was going to do, but she had expected such a hard man as he appeared to be, to protest.

'Then we won't leave him out there. Don't worry he's one of God's own creatures too,' he said in a sarcastic tone, and quickly closed the door once all three were inside. The horse's hooves clattered against the stone flagged floor. It shook its head and neck spraying them with the moist snow. Both laughed nervously as Flora brushed herself down. He soothed the animal, and Flora could see how strong the bond between them was.

'We'll tether him here, whilst I find some candles and something with which to warm ourselves. Perhaps there will be a store of altar cloths or robes in the vestry. If we're lucky there may be some bread and wine to keep our body and souls together.' He grinned broadly at her shocked face.

'Do you think it would be the right thing to do? I mean we could be accused of stealing.' She knew her point was valid, but he merely laughed at her.

'Miss, would you feel better if we died honest souls or would you like to live and use what we can to that aim. Then perhaps we could replace it when the storm abates. That would appease your conscience and we would survive. Now, I shall collect some snow in this,' he produced the communion goblet and a pewter bowl, 'That will serve as our water supply and then I shall see what we can burn to make a fire.'

'A fire! In the church?' Her words were out before she could prevent them passing her lips. But to set fire to a church — or in a church — it seemed blasphemous, or at least totally inappropriate.

'Well, in my limited knowledge of the field, I do not think one would take too well outside, miss. Have a look around and see if you can find anything that we could use to make one whilst I see to our water supply.' He raised a brow at her and reluctantly she nodded as he braced himself to open the door once more. 'Miss, even I would draw the line at bibles unless truly desperate and then I'd seek His forgiveness, but there must be something we can use to give off light or heat. See if there are any lamps.'

It was with some hesitation that she drew back the curtain to the vestry. The piercing scream that she heard caused her to stand stock still as she realised it was from her own lips that it came.

He was there in a trice. Slumped over the seat of his desk was a figure in priestly robes. 'Stay here.' Mr Simkin stepped inside. He approached the figure with caution.

'Reverend, we did not mean to trespass, however . . . ' His fingers were resting on the neck of the motionless body. He touched him but there was no movement.'

'Is he . . . dead?' Flora asked and moved forwards.

'No, but very cold. Looks as though he fell asleep and as the temperature dropped, he has been unaware of it. He placed the man's arm around his neck and was going to move him, not noticing the paper clutched in his hand.

It dropped to the floor as he was half walked, groaning, and half carried to the front pew of the church, before the altar. The man was slightly built, fortunately.

Flora and Simkin placed an assortment of robes and cloths on the rug before the altar and wrapped the man securely in them. Rubbing his hands and cheeks, Flora managed to bring some colour back into the man's face.

'Tilt his head up.' Flora did as she was told and watched as he carefully poured a little brandy into the priest's mouth. The man coughed slightly and muttered something inaudible before opening his eyes. 'The list . . . must hide the list.' The man's lids flickered momentarily and then he slipped back into oblivion. Flora held his head, carefully lowering it back on to the makeshift pillow. She turned to Mr Simkin. 'I wonder what he meant by that, the list?' But he had gone.

Flora walked back to the vestry, where a small flame was flickering, casting a light from the open arch. Inside she saw Simkin shove something into his deep pockets and then, as he heard her footsteps approaching, turned to the cupboard and pulled out a box of candles. 'Take these. Find as many candlesticks as you can and bring them all to the altar. We shall burn whatever we respectfully can.'

'What list does he mean?' Flora walked over to the priest's desk. The quill was still placed in the ink-well. But there was only a sheet of clean parchment on the desk itself, despite a smeared blotter.

'The man is delirious, miss. Can I suggest we concentrate on making ourselves as comfortable as we can and watch our charge with great care?' He handed her the box.

'You fetch them! I shall stay with the good Reverend.' Flora turned on her heel to defiantly walk away, when a hand on her shoulder stopped her mid step.

'Miss Mather, we know he is a priest. However, we do not know if he is good or bad. Please take care, Jessica, and withhold your judgment upon him until we do.'

Flora turned her head, staring at his hand upon her shoulder, and he released his grip.

'I merely advise you to take care for your own safety, miss.' He held out the candles to her. 'If you would please take these, I shall bring all else that we may need shortly.'

Flora took the candles from him. 'How do I know I can trust you? At least he is a priest; surely that should be enough.'

He smiled at her. 'Because if you couldn't or didn't trust me, you would hardly be here speaking in such a way to me now. You would be out there staying with him, wouldn't you?'

Flora did not have a chance to answer as they were both shaken by a loud thud as a door slammed open and the vestry filled with a blast of cold air.

Simkin ran into the church, a pistol drawn from inside his coat.

'Damnation, what foolery is this?' He braced himself as he ran out of the open door. The priest had gone, and the horse too. Flora gathered the discarded clothes from the floor. Wrapping an altar cloth around her she then armed herself with a candlestick, and made for the door. The snow had lain deeply. However, the tracks of three horses were fully visible.

A shot rang out but the storm still raged and Flora could not see what was happening within its depth. It was with relief that James returned. He placed an arm around her and steered her back into the church.

James bolted the door this time and immediately started to light a number of candles. He made a mound in the middle of the flagstone and, with the wooden collection plates smashed into pieces, made a fire. Warming himself, and bringing Flora close to him, he shook his head in what seemed like despair. 'The cold must have addled my brain. In all my campaigns I have never lost a horse in such a stupid way!'

'You were not to know what would have happened, Mr Simkin. He looked so ill.' She squeezed his hand to offer comfort and was surprised when he held it in between his strong, rough palms.

'My dear young lady . . . ' He looked into her eyes with a strange inquiring stare. 'He is worse than ill now. The man is dead.'

3

Flora was visibly shaken by Mr Simkin's words. He placed an arm around her as she shivered slightly.

'I'm sorry. I did not mean to shock you. I . . . I am afraid I'm more used to keeping the company of soldiers. I have forgotten, it would seem, how to address a young lady.' He held her gently, but firmly, to his side.

Flora was grateful for his warmth next to her, but felt as though she should pull herself away from him. She sat upright extricating her shoulders from the protection of his strong arm. Flora thought she caught a flash of humour cross his face but he did not stop or resist her will.

She took the attention away from the momentary awkward situation by asking, 'How can he be dead, if he was strong enough to mount a horse and ride outside in that horrendous weather? Surely he didn't just succumb to it when he could have been safe here inside with us? Are you sure he had not just fallen off your horse? He looked so weak — and perhaps we should retrieve him . . . or his . . . '

She looked towards the arched doorway and the wet area near the closed door. Moist footsteps had appeared between the door and where the priest had lain. She studied her own, and James' and realised that the marks on the old stone floor were more than theirs, just about discernable before the heat of the fire started to dry them out. At least one other person had entered the church and kidnapped the man whilst they were talking in the vestry.

She stood up as if to walk towards the now bolted door. He stopped her by tugging at her skirt's hem. Flora looked defiantly down into his deep determined eyes.

'He is dead, shot and the horse is

gone. There is only danger waiting out there for us tonight. We stay here, and keep warm and see if the weather has calmed by the morning. Then, and only then, we shall venture outside and be on our way again.'

'Shot!' Flora sat down quite quickly and hugged her knees to her, staring at the fire. 'Why? How? On a night like this no one in their right mind would be out there. Why kill a harmless priest?' Flora shook her head.

She had left one nightmare and taken herself off directly into another. How she longed for the warmth of Ivy's bakery, the smell of fresh baps and the woman's friendly loving banter. Then she remembered her step-mother and the stick she had used to hit her. Her back was still sore from her last thrashing, her one and only true beating given after her letters had been discovered.

Not that the woman could read them herself, but she had taken them to Silas who could. He had become like a man so enraged that he had shamed her throughout the village, declaring her fallen, wanton and soiled.

In the days gone by, an old woman had been burned as a witch and the fable remained within the village of Lizzie Blackmoor, but more than the infamous creature who had lived in a cave and had supposedly healed with herbs and potions and spells, was the awesome figure who was portrayed by Silas as the man who had judged and condemned her.

He had been a direct ancestor of his and was said to have died a painful death shortly afterwards. His family had always held a position of respect amongst the local folk. Silas had frightened the villagers into agreeing that Flora's punishment would be one meagre meal a day, and then silence until she was truly repentant. He would not let her talk for herself or read out her letters, her precious letters, to explain their intentions.

The fact that the letters had existed

at all was sufficient to disgrace her, and that she was prepared to run off with him was condemnation enough. Only Ivy was filled with the spirit of love sufficiently to help her. Flora would never repent of sins that only existed in the murky minds of man. Ivy had retrieved her beloved's letters, offering to burn them in her own ovens, but instead she had given them back to Flora and arranged her escape.

Flora had committed no earthly sin, not of the body, but she had fallen in love with a man from another rank of society who had promised to elope with her once he returned from the wars, but he never would.

To Silas he was a 'foreigner' from another part of the land and was not to be trusted. To Flora he was a soldier who for only too short a time had been billeted at their inn whilst helping the Customs with their problems. He was to her an honest and honourable gentleman and her love.

'You should have stayed in your

village, miss. This is no place for a young maiden. This stretch of the coast is as inhospitable as it is hostile. You would have been better where you were.' He leaned on one elbow on to the hard floor, pushing the edge of the fire with a piece of broken wood.

The small oil lamp that he had used to light the strips of cloth, kindling and oddments of parchments found by the Reverend's desk was moved back out of the way of the small flickering flames. Flora noticed, though, that James was careful to examine each piece of parchment before letting it burn. The air was filled with warmth and a heady smell.

'I would not!' Flora answered, realising she had been a little too defiant as he raised an inquisitive brow at her. 'I mean there was nowhere for me to stay. Are we safe here? Who would kidnap and shoot a priest?' Flora hugged her knees more tightly, looking around her at the dark shadowy corners of the old building. Then she stood up, this time swinging her skirts away from James and walking toward the vestry.

He quickly followed her. 'Why have you suddenly decided he was kidnapped? Where do you think you are going?'

'Look at the floor; you know more than I about tracks I'm sure. Someone else came in here and helped him out. Who killed him, Mr Simkin?' she demanded to know as she opened the large cupboard door where his robes were hung.

'I don't know but they will not be there by morning, I'm sure of that. They will have made as much space between them and their victim as possible. Whoever if was wanted to silence him.' He stood behind her as she started to remove items from the cupboards.

'What are you looking for?' he asked.

'I'm not sure. But whoever the murderer was, he had him frightened, and frightened people hide things.' She glanced back at the desk.

'I've already gone over that,' he said dryly, looking around the small room. 'So tell me, miss, what is it you are so frightened of that you would take off on your own from a quiet village in a sheltered vale and expose yourself to all of this?'

Flora turned around and stared at him. She was tired and wanted to return to the fire, but he was correct in that she was frightened and needed to be doing something to regain control over her life and her emotions. 'I merely stepped upon a coach. I had no idea that I was about to become involved in a murder or be holed up in a church with a soldier . . . '

'Retired soldier,' he corrected her.

She looked at him. 'You're a bit young to be retired aren't you?'

'My thanks, miss. I was retired early, due to an injury.' He tapped his leg.

She bent down and pulled out a box from the bottom of the cupboard. Remembering her stepmother's hiding places, she felt each plank of the base until she found one that felt slightly loose. She lifted it and found something wrapped in cloth placed carefully within the space.

With anticipation she removed what appeared to be a pistol. However, it was incomplete so she put it to the side. Beneath it lay a lamp. But even that was a sorry collapsed affair. Disappointed and tired she stood up to see James studying them keenly and holding them in his hands.

'Come back to the fire whilst we still have warmth to return to. You need to sleep, miss. Tomorrow we will have to move away from here quickly.' He stepped back allowing her to pass. He kept the items that she had found.

'Where will we report these goings on?' she asked.

'I'll see to that once you are safely delivered to your destination,' he assured her.

'Why are you keeping those broken things?' she asked, as she sat down on the front pew. He brought her some robes and an altar cloth to cover her. A kneeler served her as a pillow.

'You never know when something that looks like nothing can be of use to you. Now sleep and I'll keep watch.'

Flora looked at him a little warily. She wanted to trust him, but he was a mystery to her, yet she was so tired.

'I've checked all the doors and they are securely bolted. Sleep lady and I'll wake you when it is time to leave. No one will disturb you, rest assured.'

She looked up at him. 'No one?' she repeated.

'No one.' He winked at her and as she had nearly closed her eyes, through heavy lids, she saw him return to the vestry.

4

The next morning Flora was woken by a gentle tickling sensation on her cheek. At first she thought it was an annoying fly and tried to waft it away with her hand but, as she moved, she had the sensation of falling down. Then she remembered that it was not her bed that she was lying on as two strong arms rolled her back on to the pew and she heard his gentle laughter. 'Steady girl! The floor's hard.'

Flora opened her eyes and saw James Simkin; his face was only inches from her own. He looked tired and not at all rested. The slight lines at the corner of his eyes seemed more obvious. She sat upright and felt the stiffness in her body. She extended both arms above her head as if they were the long neck of a swan and stretched. He was staring at her.

Flora regained her composure and looked up at him as he offered her some bread and tea.

She swung her legs to the ground, making sure her skirt was properly arranged. She tucked a few wayward hairs back in place as best she could then carefully folded up the garments that had kept her warm all night. He moved his weight from his right leg to his left and then shifted it quickly back.

'Sorry,' she said for keeping him waiting.

'Old habits die hard.' He sat down next to her on the pew.

'What does that mean?' she asked, not knowing if his comment was meant to be derogatory in some way.

'I mean you have been brought up to take care of things, to work and not accept everything as your right and that is not a bad thing.' He glanced at the folded garments then smiled at her and she willingly sipped the warm brew.

'Thank you, but you weren't, were you?'

'No, miss. I wasn't, not until this gentleman became an officer. Then my eyes were opened and I learned how to become a soldier to earn the respect of men whose lives I held in my hand as much as Napoleon did on the field of battle.' He was staring at the multi-coloured window above the altar. It depicted the ascension. 'Too many die because of arrogance and ignorance.'

Flora could see a hardness cross his features. It did not sit well on such a handsome face. This man, she realised had had perhaps too many experiences of war.

'Wherever did you find such good quality tea?' Flora sipped it and was surprised by the flavour. She had helped prepare herbs that were then mixed with the quality tea that was brought at intervals to the village. With the quantity thus increased it was sold on for greater profits.

Only the richest could afford the best and most variety. Tea was just one commodity of the unseen trade; the one that everyone took their part in, but of which no one spoke openly for fear of retribution from the smuggling gangs of their own community.

Flora knew what that felt like. The militia, any soldiers who were sent to help the Customs or Excise met either open hostility or a wall of silence. Martin was different. To her he appeared almost vulnerable and did not deserve their contempt. She had never talked to him of what he referred to as the ruinous trade, but being seen talking to a soldier was enough to raise suspicion. The letters, few as they were, were proof to the ignorant of her immoral character and treacherous nature.

James' face was serious as he explained to her. 'In the store under the vestry, along with twenty-five half ankers of brandy, three rolls of tobacco and four blocks of soap.' He continued drinking his own tea from what looked like the communion goblet. She did not know if she should admire the man for his purely practical and carefree ways or whether she should be shocked by his lack of reverence.

Flora remembered how Martin had spoken to her, hoping to recover such booty. He had been so ambitious. She was deep in her own memories of Martin when the words he had spoken penetrated her thoughts. 'You mean he had all that stored here in the church? Then he too was a smuggler?'

'If he wasn't then he certainly knew some people who were, and therein lays the reason for his death. So finish your drink, the sun will be up soon and so we shall be on our way before those goods are reclaimed. I have made these to help us on our way.'

He held up what looked like dissected wicker baskets with strips of leather threaded through. 'We tie these to our boots and then we shall be able to walk on the snow more easily. The tracks from last night have been covered and are lost to us. However, we shall need to seek cover wherever possible in order to reach our destination safely.' He ruffled his hair and stared at the mark on the floor left from where he had cleared the remnants of the fire. He had placed her bag by the door.

'What about the boy?' Flora remembered the youth with the blackened eye.

'He should be well fed and sleeping soundly on a mattress. If he has any sense he will stay in his room until I can return to fetch him.' He placed the goblet down on the pew.

'Who is he to you?' she asked and saw a fleeting smile almost break out across his face.

'To me he is yet another waif I have acquired along the way. He looked pointedly at her. 'If you go in there you will find what you need to refresh yourself, then please, we need to hurry. I want us out of here before anyone comes to look for that cache.'

Flora went behind the curtain that he had pointed to, to find herself in a small storage cupboard about three feet square. There were shelves mounted on one wall to her right. On the lowest one had been placed a shallow bowl of water, a cut off the corner of a block of soap, and a small piece of clean cloth.

She smiled and took a step forward ready to freshen up her face when she kicked something on the floor. It made an empty sound, and as Flora glanced down she saw it was a chamber-pot. She put a hand to her mouth to stifle a giggle but inside she sighed with relief.

When she joined him a few moments later he had the strange contraptions on his feet and was holding hers in his hand.

'Sit down and I will tie these on for you.'

Flora sat down and he raised her foot by her ankle and placed it carefully on the contraption. He lifted the hem of her skirt so that he could see what he was doing. Flora coloured deeply. If the villagers walked in on this they would have proof enough that she was indeed beyond the pale.

He glanced up as he finished fastening one and looked almost surprised by the hue that flushed her cheeks.

'I told you I was used to soldiers and we are in the midst here of a war of a different nature. Once we are back within civilisation I shall adhere to propriety. For now just let us survive. Your other foot, miss, please?'

She lifted it up and he deftly tied on the other snow walker. For that was what she had decided they should be called. Flora sat still as he tied them firmly on and then as she stood up he steadied her when she nearly tripped over the end of one of them. She quickly learned how to take bigger strides to adapt to them.

'We have to go now.' He led the way to the door and picked up her bag. It was light as she did not possess many belongings.

'What do we do about the priest, Mr Simkin?' she asked nervously unsure about what would be seen the other side of the door away from their sanctuary.

'Don't worry; he's nowhere to be seen.' Without further explanation he led her outside.

Flora looked around anxiously, but all was like a winter's scene. If you did not know where the road should be, you would be quite lost as all was covered by a blanket of white.

'Hold my hand.' He took hold of her hand in his and she could feel how hard it was. A gentleman he may be, but this was a man who had worked too.

'Do you know where we are going?' she asked after they had crossed the fields, left the church behind them and headed for the cover of the woods.

'Yes, I do. Ebton was the name I recall.'

His answer was short and he had returned to being sarcastic once more. This was a trait that Flora found to be quite annoying as he was toying with her again like a cat does with a mouse.

'I meant, have you been here before?

Do you know the area, the people? Is it your home?' They stepped between two trees and entered the cold heart of the woodland.

His eyes seemed to look everywhere. Then he looked down at her slightly flustered face.

'Yes, I have been here before, and I know some of the people and it is one of my homes. Now may we continue in silence so as to not wake up everyone within a mile of us, or would you prefer to sit here and freeze whilst we chat?' He put a hand out to gesture that they should continue.

Flora lowered her voice to a whisper. 'You, sir, have no manners, you have spent too much time in the company of soldiers and have quite forgotten how to address a lady!'

She stepped out in front of him following in the direction he had pointed to.

'Very possibly, but then you, my dear, are no lady.'

She turned around immediately forgetting to allow for her basket shoes and fell forward.

He caught her in his open arms and held her firmly. 'You were saying?'

'Unhand me, sir!' She was struggling to sort her feet out and leaning on him as she did so.

'If I do, Flora, you will land on your . . .'

Flora pulled herself upright centring her balance. A cold feeling of anger engulfed her. She stared at him in fury and defiance. 'How dare you?' She pointed at him with her finger. He looked at it wide-eyed, obviously and infuriatingly humoured by all she said and did. The man was quite impossible.

'If I hadn't caught you, girl, you would have fallen on your face. Would you have preferred that? It may have cooled your hot-headed temper.'

'You called me Flora! You called me Flora!' she said, and pulled her bag from his hand. 'How could you?' Flora was infuriated and shamed once more as she had been found out. He must have gone through her bag and read her letters whilst she slept. No wonder he thought nothing of playing with her ankles and treating her so.

He knew she had been prepared to elope with a soldier, a junior officer. Would everyone in Christendom soon know their contents? She wished she had had the strength of character or the quickness of mind to burn them in his fire. Now he would think of her as a low-life, a liar, and he had already heard what her mother-in-law had called her by the coach.

It hurt her deeply. She thought she would never care again what another soul thought of her, but in her heart she knew she did. She wanted this man's respect and she had lost it through her own deceit.

'It's your name, woman. Be proud of it and stop hiding behind homespun lies. You are no good at them; you do not have the essence of a liar in your heart. So cheer up and be glad, and let us be on our way before we are caught in the next storm.' He stepped around her ready to lead the way.

Without a further word he took the bag back from her hand and with one finger placed it to her lips, to tell her to say no more, then walked on. She was expected to follow, and feeling like a rebuked child she did.

They continued for a few miles. Progress was slow, the air was freezing and Flora felt colder than ever she had in her whole life. When he reached a point at the edge of a ridge, they could look down a slope through the trees and in distance could see an expanse of sea. Between them and the hamlet lay a good four or five miles of open snow covered country. Flora felt light-headed, and her knees as though they were about to buckle beneath them.

He placed his arm around her. Her head told her to pull away. However, her heart wanted to stay next to his, warm and secure with his strength.

'We'll go to that small barn and rest there. You cannot complete the journey today and it would not be safe for me to leave you there on your own.' He helped her down the steep slope to the lower wood and then to the field where the barn stood.

'I'm sorry if I have slowed you down. I did not mean to be a burden to you.'

'Then you should have stayed with Frederick, as I told you do.' His reply was instant.

'Go ahead then, I'll be fine here on my own.' They entered the old building.

'You deserve to be left for a reply like that. However, you would die if I did, so I shall not, but remember you wished to make this journey. Therefore, do not complain about the company you keep.'

He placed her bag down beside her and moved around three bales of hay into an open sided square shape. 'Settle into the middle there. I shall make a shelter to ward off some of the cold and try to light a small fire to keep us warm.'

'I'm sorry,' Flora said after she had had time to calm down. 'I didn't think it would take us this long to arrive at Ebton, and I knew once you were gone you would not be able to make it back the next morning to the inn. I cannot afford to stay at inns and I was scared that I might be left there deserted. Or if we had been taken on to a place the size of Newcastle I would have been desolate. I've never left the village or vale before. I thought I'd be safe if I travelled to Ebton with you.'

'Well, I suppose at least you did a lot of thinking. However, you are here now and we need to stay warm.' He lit a small fire using the broken pistol that created a flare once triggered.

'I didn't think it would work.' Flora looked at it in amazement. He then unfolded the apparently broken light and it became a fully working lamp.

'They are some of the tools of the trade, Flora; used to signal to the cobles and cutters offshore when a landing is to be made. Caught with these on us and the tea that I borrowed from the church store we would be suspected of involvement instantly.'

Flora opened her bag and removed the parcel that Ivy had wrapped for her. The bread and pie still smelt fresh and she saw a look of delighted surprise on James' face which puzzled her.

The letters were wrapped apparently as she had left them under the stiffener at the base of the bag, so had he read them or not? If not, how would he know who she was?

'You are a lady full of surprises — some are pleasant ones, miss,' he said, as he gratefully took half of the food which she offered to him.

Flora ate gladly and thought just how full of surprises Mr Simkin was too.

5

It was a cold desolate place and there was no respite in the storm. Flora hugged herself tightly as she watched James build up a bigger fire in the centre of the barn.

She stepped from one foot to the other as the snow had melted and the water penetrated the worn out leather of her boots. Sparks flew as the draught, or more she thought — wind, whistled through the run-down building's walls. Mr Simkin seemed to be used to setting and managing the flames to obtain a greater blaze and warmer effect.

'I hope your horse is safe,' Flora commented, trying to keep the conversation off more personal matters. 'Do you think we'll get back to your friend, Frederick, before the end of the week?'

'Campion will be too valuable to

them to injure him deliberately.' He determinedly prodded the fire's embers with a piece of iron he had found in the corner of the barn. It looked like part of a broken branding iron. 'Frederick will at least be warm and well fed and, so long as he stays in his room, he should be safely out of trouble's reach.'

'Them? You mean there was more than one man out last night? We were only in the vestry for such a short time yet heard nothing until the door banged shut.' Flora tried to camouflage the surprise in her voice.

She should have realised that it would take more than a single man to both lift the priest and control the horse, but this was so far removed from her very narrow experience of life that she found the whole prospect that they had been so near to murderers frightening.

He looked at her and nodded. 'You must have been aware of the trade within your village. It is rife throughout the whole region from Newcastle down to Hull and beyond. Neither the excise officers or the riding officers of the customs force can pin them down and stop it.' He twiddled with the iron rod, spinning it in his fingers, but she knew he was watching her closely.

'Well everyone knows about it, but they also choose to know nothing. It doesn't pay to ask too much about other folks' business. Seeing anything or being witness to movements and noises after dark can be very dangerous; bad for one's health is how they put it. You learn to turn the other way. Most of the villagers are good people.'

She spoke softly feeling odd to be defending the very people who had turned on her and made her an outcast. Except for Ivy, she had a good heart and was different to most of the people there. Perhaps it was because she was a daughter of Ebton who had married into their community and was therefore used to being considered an outsider, even after twenty years.

'I mean things are priced so high

because of the duties, that normal folk can't buy them. That's not fair, is it?' Flora noticed his grip tightened on the rod and she wondered if she had been far too outspoken for him.

'Miss, where do you think the coin paid for the contraband goes to?' He tilted his head on one side as she considered his question.

'To their suppliers, I suppose.' Flora had never given the matter any thought before. It was just a part of daily life to be grateful for anything that came their way.

'To the French, Flora. It goes to Napoleon's war effort. He needs our gold and people around here supply it. Without even thinking or caring they pay for the enemy's soldiers that their own brothers, husbands, sons . . . or lovers face on the field of battle.'

She stared at him as he said 'lovers', images of Martin flashed across her mind. Her cheeks flushed and her temper rose.

'No, miss, it is not an innocent trade,

it is a murderous one that is like a disease throughout our society and its effects are paid not here, but by our own countrymen across the seas in foreign lands.'

'Are you a customs officer, Mr Simkin?' Flora stared at him. His face was deathly serious and his deep blue eyes held her glare as he answered.

'No, miss, not directly, but I am a retired soldier and I, like many others, see this business for what it is — a cowardly, merciless trade that needs to be stopped. Men can live without brandy, geneva, tea and silks, not to mention other lesser commodities. But we must beat Napoleon, and soon.' He threw the iron rod to one side as Flora visibly shivered.

'I did not mean to lecture you. It must be the cold making me boorish. Come closer, miss, and then you shall be warm. I'll not harm you.'

He rubbed his left leg as he shuffled nearer to her around the back of the fire. Hesitantly she moved next to him.

'We shall be here until the weather breaks. We can use the hay to cover us and we shall use our own body heat to keep ourselves warm. Do not fear me, Flora. I am your friend, you will be safe.' He placed an arm around her and pulled her next to him. She nearly moved away from him, but he whispered to her like a mother comforting a child. 'Don't. Stay warm and be safe.'

Flora nestled herself down, but he felt her arm and shook his head. 'That coat is soaked through, so are your boots. Whatever possessed you to venture out in such weather so ill equipped?'

'I had no choice about leaving or about the clothes I wore. My selection of attire is somewhat limited.' She sat upright offended by his manner.

'Take off your coat and boots. I'll use the hay and the heat from the fire to try to dry them off somewhat.'

'I'll freeze!' she said, amazed that he should suggest such a thing.

He removed the greatcoat and for the

first time she saw his uniform. She sat there mesmerised, memories flowing back to her, for it reminded her of her lieutenant, her Martin. Only this man was of a higher rank. He was a major.

She removed her cold, wet coat and handed it to him. He wrapped her in the greatcoat, which was warm and dry on the inside. For the first time since leaving the bakery she felt warm. She removed her boots and tucked her feet up under her skirts. He packed each boot with hay and lay them down to the side of the fire, but away from the direct heat.

'When they have dried off I'll put some soldier's friend on them.'

She looked at him. 'Soldier's friend?' she queried.

'It's a mixture of oil and wax. I always carry a small tin of it with me. It covers a multitude of uses and needs.'

His coat was far too big for her, but she felt secure and warm wrapped in its heavy fabric.

'Did you know a soldier called

Lieutenant Martin Fforbes?' she asked warily.

He came back to her once he had packed out her coat and spread it over some bales. The moisture started to rise from its hem that was nearest the fire.

He rested his hands on top of his knees as he sat down next to her.

'Yes, I knew him. He was in my regiment and died courageously, many years before he should have.' He placed a hand on her shoulder. 'I know he intended to return to your village and had foolish dreams of eloping with a young maid.' He dipped his head so that he could look her straight in the eye.

'Why foolish? Have you never been in love before?' She swallowed hard as this man, this major, was hard and she had no wish to cry like a baby in front of him.

'He would have destroyed his career, wrecked his future and lost his inheritance. All that just for 'love'.' He picked up the iron bar and returned to poking the fire once more.

'You are cynical, sir, and have possibly been in the wars too long. Have you never been in love?' She repeated her question and noticed how he fidgeted uneasily before rubbing his left leg once more.

'That is of no concern to you. I know love to be a folly. A poor man soon loses his dreams of romance. Empty bellies to feed soon sobers a man's mind. Martin was a dreamer, not made for the life of a soldier, more befitting the whim of an artist. However, he was brave and honourable and, Miss Flora Merryman, he would have come to you if he were able and honour whatever promises he had made.'

He offered her his kerchief, but she would not take it. She swallowed again and shook her head. 'If you want to help to prevent other young hearts from being needlessly broken them help me. It was I who forwarded Martin's last pay and his letter to your friend, Ivy. He asked me to and I honoured his wishes. He knew you would be hounded out of the village if your plans had become known.'

Flora listened in silence.

'Ivy returned the message of thanks and told me you were disclosed. That is why you were sent to take this coach. I promised to see you safely to Ebton, but my motives are not only driven by a duty to my young friend, but also to my countrymen. I need your help.'

'Help you to do what?' Flora was very suspicious of him. He had known who she was all along and most likely that it was her own stepmother who had called her those names.

'Help me to crush the trade. Tell me all you know of the goings on in the village — in particular that of Silas Diggle.'

Flora looked at him wide-eyed. She knew the penalty for being a traitor to her own kind, but if the money was funding Napoleon's army then she owed it to Martin to do all she could to stop it. Either way the only thing she had to lose was herself — her own life. She stared at the flames unable to answer him.

6

Flora fell silent. She was unaware that she knew anything of significance about the smugglers and the happenings in the village. She had always tried to turn her head and look the other way, as she had been brought up to.

'Have you any more food in your bag, Flora?' he asked her as she had not been forthcoming with a response from his previous plea.

'Yes, a little.' She was loathe to move as she had finally warmed through, wrapped up in his greatcoat by the fire, and her feet had temporarily stopped aching with the cold. 'Please, help yourself. It is wrapped up in a cloth on the top of my things.'

He picked up her bag and opened it. She watched him look carefully inside. He removed the cloth wrapped bread, but then instead of fastening the bag

James stared back inside it. Flora became very uneasy. 'That's all the food I have in your hand. There is no more, honestly.'

He looked at her and smiled. 'I realise that. I'm just amazed you bother to carry the bag at all. The contents hardly seem to warrant it!' He closed it and placed it back on the floor, then glanced back at Flora.

She was near to tears, but swallowed to keep her composure. Flora was stifling her feelings of despair at her situation. She knew that she needed to grieve for Martin, feeling the urge to walk out into the open air, and to be free. Not to be holed up in such a place with a stranger surrounded by a blanket of freezing white. This was not the adventure or future she had planned with Martin. It was to have been far grander, warmer and exciting.

He changed the position of her boots and the threadbare coat, then seated himself next to her, but he was careful of the way in which he placed his left leg. She saw him wince as he tried to take the weight from it and sat down.

'Flora, I apologise — again. Sometimes I speak before thinking of the insults that I unintentionally inflict upon you. Your poverty is nothing to be ashamed or nor, I suppose, is your condition. It can happen to any young woman who has had her head turned by a gallant young soldier. You will, rest assured, be cared for. So you must not worry about the future, just concentrate on your current situation.' He squeezed her shoulder with his hand and her mouth dropped open slightly. His patronising manner was more than she could bear.

'Just think, Flora. If you tell me all you know of the people who come and go from the village, you will be helping yourself. Think about what goods appear in the night, the coming and going of wagons, carts, and tubmen. Who is the master smuggler? The link man has to be someone who travels around but is local, who can work out all the pick-ups and distribution net-work. Could it be Silas?' He stared at her.

Although Silas was a devious and powerful man Flora did not know if it was him.

'The extra money you will earn could secure the future of you and your child. You could have a life worth living.' He was looking into her hazel eyes as if trying to reach her very soul with his words.

'How dare you! What do you think I am?' She stood up, staring down at him as he leaned casually back against the hay. He was handsome, arrogant and patronising and she would have left him there if only it had been possible.

'They turned you out. You have nothing to fear from them. You owe them nothing, Flora. Your silence and everyone else's protects the ruinous trade and the traitors who perpetrate it. Think of Martin, work with me for him.' He was twiddling with a piece of hay as he spoke to her.

'How dare you accuse me of being with child!' Flora was incensed.

He lifted an eyebrow as her words were shouted directly at him.

'You mean you are not? Did you lie to snare him?' He gave the appearance of being genuinely puzzled.

She picked up her boots and pulled out the damp hay that had been packed within them.

'I did not lie. I did not tell him any such thing, as he knew it was not possible. Martin was a gentleman, sir, something you are not and shall never be.'

She pulled on the boots and grabbed her bag. Without realising she was still wearing his coat she opened up the barn door and saw sheets of white flakes still falling on to a blanket covering the ground and the temperature chilled her skin. She felt the bag slip from her fingers and the door was closed in front of her. Dazed, she was turned around and walked back to the fire.

She felt two strong arms encircle her and then it happened — she cried, like she had never cried before, because she had lost her dream and her future, and her present seemed as bleak as the weather. It was only when he laid her back against the hay and pulled off her boots, replacing them and filling them with new hay that she realised what he had been doing.

He brought her some of Ivy's bread. 'Here, have a sip of this and eat the bread? You need all your strength.'

She looked at the small flask that he was offering her and after rubbing her eyes on the back of her hand she took a swig of the fine brandy within it. 'You did that on purpose. You knew I was not with child, you just wanted me to break down in front of you. I hope you are happy now but it was a cruel trick.'

'Perhaps it was, Flora. I shall not apologise for it because you needed to let some of your grief and despair out. Now, you can be strong and show me your determination to make a future, but until the tears had been shed you would have continued to spend your energy and resolve in fighting them. So let this go now, as soon as you can, and live your life free of the past.'

For the first time she saw his face relax and a genuine smile appeared, peeling back the years. The brandy had affected them both, or was it that for the first time the tension between them had dissipated?

'Do you forgive me now, or am I still to be considered a blackguard?' He placed his hand inside his jacket and produced a small bottle. He held it in the palm of his hand as if considering whether to ask her something or not. Then he replaced it, and looked the other way.

'I forgive you this once.' Flora did feel lighter in spirit as if she had released the emotions that had threatened to bring her to her knees as they had struggled through the storm. 'Is there something you need me to do,

Major Simkin?' she asked, and saw the colour in his cheeks rise. The hard soldier had a gentler and more vulnerable side also, she thought.

'I'm retired, no more a serving major. I have not returned to my civilian clothes, that is all, but I shall as soon as I am home; and the answer to your questions is yes. I need you to look at my wound and make sure that it is not . . . ' he cleared his throat.

'Infected? Bad?' she offered as he nervously fumbled for the right word. One that she suspected frightened him more than a Frenchman with a sabre would. 'It has been bothering you since we rode to the church, hasn't it?'

'Yes, but it is not something a gentleman would ask a lady to do, miss.' He smiled a little impishly at her.

'We have established that you are not a gentleman, and clearly I am of humble birth and used to looking after folk, so show me your wound and let us see how big a mess we are really in, for there is no surgeon in these parts.'

His head shot around at the mention of a sawbones.

She winked at him and he sighed. 'That was very cruel,' he answered.

'Then we are equal for once, sir.'

He nodded the turned his back to her as he unbuttoned his breeches.

'Once you are sorted we can hopefully get some sleep, for I fear I am in need of some,' Flora said calmly by way of a distraction but thought her words were ill chosen as he lowered his breeches. His shirt hung low covering his leg to muscular mid thigh, but there beneath the hemline was a poorly wrapped stained cloth bandaging his leg.

He untied it and the cloth fell to the ground. Flora tossed it on to the fire. A cut at least four inches in length ran down the back of his leg above the knee. It looked sore and angry, but there was no sign of discolouration.

'It has been aggravated, but with your

ointment and a new bandage it should be fine.'

Flora rubbed on the ointment then wrapped a piece of fabric ripped from his shirt hem around the leg. Quickly he replaced his clothes and stood proud. He had let her see the vulnerability of his fear as if in understanding of her own.

'Now we sleep, Miss Flora, and in the morning a new day will dawn for both of us.' He insisted she kept his coat and he said he used her own as a blanket as she slept.

'You must sleep also, now that you know your leg is safe.' She moved over slightly making room for him.

He lay next to her and she spread the coats across both of them. 'Major . . .'

'James, please,' he said as he lay still next to her.

'I will help you, but it will not be easy,' Flora said quietly.

He squeezed her hand. 'Thank you, I will personally see that you are safe.'

'And who will protect you, Major James?'

He was silent for a moment. 'The law, Miss Flora, and the dragoons.'

'Then we have a bigger battle to fight than I think you anticipate.'

7

The sound of the door creaking awoke Flora. This was swiftly followed by a blast of cold air sweeping across the barn's hay-strewn floor. She sat bolt upright, James had gone, the fire was blown out and the door was flapping loose in the wind.

She was still wearing his greatcoat, so reasoned that he could not be far away. Flora plunged her hands into the deep coat pockets to protect them from the cold.

She felt something inside and pulled it out. It was a piece of parchment tucked into an inside pocket. She recognised it as the one that had been in front of the priest. So James had not burned it but had kept it safe.

Flora had been taught her letters by her real ma, enough to recognise a list of names. Holding it to the daylight, she read the first one: *Ellerby, Pummel, Fforbes, Merryman and Frederick S*. The name of her Martin and Frederick S — Simkin? They both had a line crossed through them. She paused, her hand started to shake as she saw her own name listed. What did her Martin's name have to do on a list miles from where he fell?

Was she implicated with him? Did they already think she had been telling him all the local secrets regarding the trade, when in fact they had spoken of nothing other than of themselves, and their own future? He had asked her about her family and the villagers, but her life was so removed from his own lifestyle that it had appeared to be no more than innocent curiosity.

Flora swallowed because the more she reflected upon those conversations the more she realised she had divulged some of the secrets of the kith and kin of the village. What had appeared to be innocent chatter had possibly been clever probing by a man working for the customs service. For the first time she doubted her own judgement, but worse than that, she questioned Martin's initial interest in her.

James had told her he was honourable so she did not doubt that he had then fallen in love with her, but still she felt as though her naivety had placed both of them in great danger. Something did not make any sense to her. Was this Frederick, the boy who had gone to the inn? If so, he too was a Simkin.

She could not make sense of it. Who were the Simkins? She folded it back over and saw that on the reverse of it was the name *Silas*. Flora gasped. If he was a party to these people she knew how deeply she was in trouble.

Carefully she returned it to the place where it had been hidden and ran outside the barn. She was determined to find out what it was that she had become mixed up in and who exactly James and Frederick were.

The storm had stopped and the sun's

rays were at last shining through the broken clouds. The countryside was glistening, covered by a blanket of white, hardly disturbed by man or beast. Flora could see that the door had been repeatedly pushed against the snow drift to force it open. A solitary set of footprints led the way around the back of the barn.

Flora followed them, recognising from the shape that they were made by James' boots. It seemed strange to think she had slept beside the man, someone she hardly knew yet, despite herself she trusted him. Flora must have been so tired because she had hardly been aware of him there at all.

She took overly large steps, placing her foot in each one of James'. He had oiled the leather of her boots and they were once more dry and warm but she did not want to risk burying them into the deep virgin snow straightaway, destroying them again.

Flora could not see where the footsteps led once she had entered the cover of the woodland from which they had arrived the day before. She peered into the gloom but saw no sign of movement. There were only two options that she could think of; she would have to shout for him or be prepared to wait in the barn hoping he would soon return to her. Then remembering the events of the previous day, she hesitated as she opened her mouth to call James but stopped herself in case they were not alone.

A sharp movement at her side made her lose her footing; swiftly Flora was pulled off her feet. She landed on top of James. He quickly rolled her off him on to the snow. Placing a warning finger to her lips he faced her.

'What is amiss?' she asked in a barely audible whisper.

'I have been through the woods and there is movement on the other side. They are distributing the goods. Stay here a while. I was going to come back and fetch both you and your bag when you decided to go for a stroll!' His words were quiet but his annoyance with her was most evident.

'I was looking for you? There are questions you must answer and . . . ' She glared at him as he shushed her. He shook his head.

'Woman your sense of timing is abysmal! Have you not the sense to stay safe, warm and dry?'

Flora was going to protest. However, he stopped her by covering her mouth with his hand. 'Lay here still and I shall return shortly with your bag then we shall make our way swiftly to the outskirts of Ebton.'

Flora was so tempted to bite his palm, but sense prevailed and she laid there still, until he returned to her.

Without saying a further word he gestured to her that they should change back into their own coats and that she should follow behind him.

She wanted to know why they were planning on going only to the outskirts of Ebton. Had he decided she could make her way from that point and then he would leave her and eventually make his way back to Frederick? Her head was filled with unasked questions and she suspected that as far as James was concerned they could remain unanswered.

Her name was on the list. Whoever had crossed off Martin's name had also decided to cross off Frederick's. The boy had a bruise on his face. She doubted that James had been the perpetrator of such a blow so it made sense to her that he had somehow saved the youth. Had word got back to them that he was dead? It was a possibility. Then why was the priest murdered?

If he was working with them, why should they kill him? The more she thought about events the more she was sure that James held the key to what was going on. Once they stopped she would have the matter out with him or refuse to go into the village. Then she was certain he would have to share his secret with her or she would be a thorn in his side.

She struggled to keep pace with him as they skirted the woodland, making their way down towards the coast. He stopped periodically to wait for her and from the look he gave her and the clenched fist at his side, she realised that perhaps she already was.

When they finally stopped trudging their way along through the cold wintry day they stopped by a huge ornate pair of iron gates. They had walked along the snow covered road with their tattered snow-walkers still tied to their boots; at least they prevented them from slipping and falling. For nearly a mile they had been skirting around what appeared to be the stone wall of a large estate.

She had fallen into step silently behind James, her mind filled with so many unanswered questions. They whirled around her brain but no one came to the fore, so Flora hardly knew where to begin confronting James about any of them.

He stopped and peered through the black painted gates.

Flora looked inside the grounds. At the end of a long curving drive was built a fine manor house. From the smaller windows, uneven brick and high chimneys she could tell it was quite old. 'How can people live like that when there are so many lacking food nearby?'

'Oh, I suspect the answer is easily. Once you are born to such a life it is seen as your right. We all have our crosses to bear.' He patted her shoulder and she peered up at him. He was toying with her again. She knew he thought her naïve of the world, and in truth she had to admit that she was.

It annoyed her, though, that he found her serious comments and beliefs frivolous. He was patronising but, as she knew only too well, he was a man — a gentleman himself, so what better was she to expect. 'Do we stop here and ask them for help?' Flora inquired.

'We stop here.' He winked at her and then turned the large ornate handle releasing the catch that held the two gates shut. Putting his shoulder to them, he pushed against one gate to try to force it open against the blown snowdrift that had wedged it shut. Obviously no one had come or gone through them since the storm had arrived.

Flora saw him grimace as he placed his weight on his left leg. 'Be careful of your wound, James!' She pushed her way in front of him and moved the gate slowly open. After a few moments she had made a large enough gap for her to squeeze her body through.

She slipped inside and looked around for a stick which she used to clear away some of the snow from the ground to allow it to open sufficiently for James to squeeze through too. When she looked up Flora saw him standing there, relaxed, with his arms folded and a wide smile upon his face.

'What?' she asked, raising the stick in

her hand, then shrugged her shoulders, not understanding what was humouring him so. 'I am glad you find my efforts amusing.'

'It is the first time I have ever been rescued by a fair damsel.' He took a step forward and slid between the gates.

Flora flung the stick away. 'Well, Mr Simkin, be grateful that I'm here then. My hair is far from fair, by the way,' Flora answered confidently and was surprised when he placed his arm around her shoulders and walked alongside her.

'Oh, I am, heartily. But, dear sweet Flora, it is your character, like your skin that is fair, although your hair may be as dark and rich as the purest and finest brew.'

He squeezed her shoulder lightly, swinging her bag carelessly in his other hand. He appeared to be very relaxed about this place. 'Call me James, please. I like the sound of it from your lips.' He winked at her and she blushed which caused his smile to broaden even wider, then he eagerly looked ahead towards the manor.

'Is that a witch's brew, you refer to?' she asked whimsically, but could not help to think of Silas and reflect upon the tales of the village's dark past.

'No, not of witches, but strong tea, expensive varieties. It was a poor comparison as they are not all brown, but I am not an artist or poet. Just take the compliment as it was intended. I believe you have had too few in your life and that, Flora, is a real shame.'

Flora stared at him, her face felt extremely hot against the cold air, and she knew she was deeply embarrassed. Martin had uttered many a smooth compliment, it was natural to him, but with James, the effort it took him to think of the correct words made the rare gesture so much more touching and personal. He was a mystery. 'You have more layers than an onion, Mr Simkin,' she replied.

'James,' he said softly. 'So long as I do not smell quite so bad as one.'

'James,' she replied in a hardly audible tone, deciding that she liked the sound of his name also. The scar on his neck made him look so severe when he was serious, yet, in those moments when he let an inner James surface he had the manner of a fun-loving young gentleman; unlike Martin, who was more studious and theological in his ideas.

James had an inner passion that flowed like a river as it twisted and turned on the way to the sea, sometimes slow moving and calm, at others, rushing, almost desperate — always strong and determined upon its course. Flora liked him, yet he had so much depth she doubted she could ever truly know him.

8

As they made their way up to the manor doors, he shared the burden of his weight on her and she realised just how much his leg pained him.

She helped him climb the steps up to the main door. There was a huge ornate ring-pull by the side. He stood proud, releasing her shoulder and pulled the ring firmly.

'Do you know the owners of this place, James?' she asked in a lowered voice.

'Yes . . . very well.' He smiled warmly at her.

The door opened and an aged manservant stared at her, then saw James' face and instantly gasped aloud. He stepped forward and gave him an emotional hug. 'Oh dear Lord, Master James.' The old man withdrew from his embrace, blushing and offering his sincere apologies for his emotionally charged behaviour.

He brushed James' uniform down with his hand as if he had defiled it. 'Master James, I forgot myself. I was quite overcome. Do forgive me, Sir.'

'Giles, you do not need me to forgive you for such a warm greeting, unless of course you intend to leave us out here permanently, freezing on the doorstep.' James was leaning casually against the door frame.

The old servant's actions were swift for his age. He ushered them both inside, leading them straight into a morning room where the fire was already lit.

'Oh, Major, we heard that you had been taken down, injured and no one knew if you lived or not. Your poor brother has been beside himself; he has not known if you lived or perished on the field like your dear cousin, Mr Martin, bless his soul.' Giles shook his head and stared momentarily down at the floor.

The old man was obviously deeply moved by James' sudden appearance, but Flora stared directly at James. He was the cousin of her Martin! He had never said. James did not look at her but, almost as if intentionally done, he kept his eyes from meeting her gaze.

'Well, I am here now so you can tell Timothy, please, and then we shall be reunited. He will not have to worry about me anymore. Or perhaps I should go to him and surprise him.'

The old man looked at him. 'No, no, Sir. I shall be more than able to. Sir, do you wish me to remove . . . those?' He pointed at their snow-walkers and both James and Flora instantly bent down to remove them. They had been so relieved to enter a warm house that neither had thought for a moment about removing them or their snow-covered boots.

James collected them up and gave them to Giles. 'Throw the contraptions away, Giles. Fetch me some dry footwear and something suitable for my friend. Also, she needs some dry clothes if it could be arranged. Jessica's may fit her perhaps?'

Giles held the wet items as if they were offensive. 'Yes, Sir, of course. I think her dresses will be a little roomy but they should still fit . . . miss?' He paused but James did not offer him her name or an introduction. Giles continued regardless, 'You did know about your cousin's death, Sir, didn't you?'

'Yes, Giles, I did. I was with him when he was shot.' He glanced at Flora, as if he had slipped up and said something out of turn. 'He died with courage and dignity.' James stared at the man Giles with an unusual intensity and Flora was sure he was trying to tell him not to ask any further questions upon the subject.

'Mr Martin, Sir?' Giles repeated, as if James' latter comment was questionable.

Flora had a peculiar feeling that made her stomach flinch.

'Yes, Giles. Now please inform my brother that I am here and fetch a warm cloak for my friend . . . Miss Flora Merryman!' His tone had changed, it was more severe and the older man nodded understanding.

Flora wondered what the two of them knew that she did not.

Giles looked at her as if for the first time and muttered underneath his breath, 'Yes, Sir, I shall do that, immediately.' He left them in the ornately decorated room and shut the cream coloured doors using the gold covered handles.

'You are Martin's cousin? Why did it not occur to you to mention it? What else are you not mentioning to me, sir, or is that . . . Sir.' She dipped a curtsey at him then placed her hands on her hips, defiant and challenging, with her colour rising.

He stood directly in front of her, his arms folded apparently casually, yet again, across his chest. She thought he did that to distance himself from people, it was a habit she had noted that he had. He looked severe again, but his eyes still betrayed a softer side. His manner was slowly changing towards her.

'Yes, Flora, he was my cousin. Yes, I thought it an irrelevant fact to mention until we were safe and dry. Then we could talk the whole affair through. However, it was our survival that occupied my mind on our journey and not the tittle-tattle of family trees. Now, can I suggest that you do not stand like that; it makes you look like a farmer's wife!'

Flora dropped her hands to her side, flustered. 'As I recall the weather was fine when I entered the coach, yet, you played a game of cat and mouse with me. Our survival was not an issue then, now was it?' She paused and raised a brow thinking she had made a valid point and caught him off guard.

'It was not the weather, Flora, that was threatening our survival, but mankind; or cretin members of the species. Now, trust me as you have so far and we shall be fine.' He let his hands drop to his side.

'Well now that we are here you can talk to me freely. So talk!' She snapped back at him, but not in a loud voice because she was becoming ever more aware of the luxury of her surroundings, and just how far they were from her humble cottage.

'Later . . . over dinner. I'll arrange it so that we can have some time to ourselves. But I will tell you this.' He placed a hand on her shoulder, and looked directly into her eyes. She glanced at his hand but he did not remove it. 'This is my home. I lived here from birth to going to school, Cambridge and then to war. I was happy here, not knowing or caring who dug out a living from the estate grounds or who starved when crops beyond my walls failed. But, that was before the war, I grew up here in a physical sense.

'I believed my privilege of place to be my God given right; that was what I was brought up to believe. However, times and people change. I have changed and so shall things around here. I shall not apologise for it, because it is the way my family and many other landed gentry think, but my life has been much changed.'

She glanced at his hand again, so casually rested upon her, her attitude still slightly indignant, but not knowing what to say to his sudden confession.

He squeezed her shoulder gently before removing his hand, then sat down in his favourite chair. 'My name is Sir James Richmond-Simkin, but you may still call me James.' He had the same menacing expression on his face that he had had on the coach when he had teased her.

'Will you ever tell me the truth, James?' She looked at him and stood in front of both him and the fire.

'That is my title, I swear it on my dear mama's grave.' He sounded almost hurt that she should not believe him.

'I mean the truth about Martin. I

never doubted your position among the gentry as you have their in-born arrogance . . . '

He laughed openly at her comment.

She continued unabated, 'There is something you are keeping from me, and don't deny it!' She squatted down by his knee. 'I deserve to know. Did Martin dupe me? Have I been a fool? You said he was going to come back to me. Did you lie, Sir?' Flora placed a hand upon his knee, desperate to be told the truth.

'The truth is not always what we want to hear.' His expression had changed, and her heart felt heavy as she realised that whatever it was, all was not as she would have it be.

'I must know.' She looked imploringly at him.

He covered her hand with his own stroking it gently. 'Then, Flora, when we are bathed, changed and fed, I shall tell you all. But you will have to be strong.'

Flora stared at him in silence, for her

world that had changed so much in such a short time was about to take another turn and she suspected it was not going to be one she found easy to accept.

9

A maid returned to escort Flora up the old oak staircase opposite the entrance hall. The walls were hung with life-size portraits of the former owners. Flora paused on the upper landing to stare at one of James and his brother, she presumed. He was tall and quite slender as a youth with fairer hair and complexion, unlike James' taller and more athletic build.

'This way, miss,' the maid said, and led her towards a large door. The bedchamber seemed vast to Flora. The ceiling was so high and a four poster bed took pride of place against a panelled wall in the Jacobean house. She stared around her in awe. The floor space in the room covered a larger area than the whole of the cottage she had been raised in, and that had slept five people.

Through the window Flora could see a vast white landscape. She looked down and saw that over a chaise-lounge was draped a pale lemon and white floral print dress. The pattern was very delicate although the fabric itself looked quite thick and warm and the stitching was extremely fine. Undergarments were laid out upon the rich red fabric cover that covered the bed. There were more pieces displayed than she had ever realised that ladies wore.

Flora walked slowly over to the dress; the sleeves were puffed around the shoulder but then they were designed to hug the arm to a low wrist. The fitted bodice was edged by a delicate lace collar, tucking neatly to a line underneath the chest, the skirt hung long and sleek. The whole garment was made with skill and of excellent quality.

'Ma'am, I've put you some fresh warm water, soap petals and a towel on the stand next to the bed. Do you wish me to help you to wash and prepare for dinner, miss?' The girl was looking at her, wide-eyed.

Flora realised she was completely out of her depth. She looked at the garments on the bed, and noticed a pair of white silk pumps on the floor. They were slightly worn but, as she turned them over in her hands, she admired the fine stitching of the embroidered flowers that decorated their top.

She thought they were totally impractical for about almost every daily task she had ever undertaken. On an earthen floor they would not have lasted an hour, but on the highly polished and richly carpeted floors of this manor house they were adequate.

'Miss?' The maid shut the door behind them and walked over to where Flora was standing, still speechless. 'Miss, sit yourself down on the chair and I'll pull off your 'dirties' and we'll prepare you to meet Sir James at dinner.'

'I'm sorry, I was not deliberately ignoring you, it's just that I've walked a long way, my feet are cold and ache and I'm rather tired.' Flora smiled at the girl.

'Look, we haven't got time to get you a bath, but you stay still and I'll have you as fresh as a daisy in no time. Now, how about I fetch you a nice hot drink of chocolate from the kitchen first? Then we'll soak those aching feet of yours whilst I sort the rest of you out, eh, miss?' The girl pulled over a chair to her and sat her down on it.

'I'm not useless you know!' Flora exclaimed and then seated herself. She did not mean to snap at the girl, it was just that she was used to 'doing' for others and all this attention and finery felt so strange.

'I'm sorry, miss. I was trying to help.' The maid apologised and stepped back as if she had been dismissed.

'It is I who am sorry. I am tired.' The girl nodded at her and left.

Flora had never had the drink before but the word 'hot' had her mouth watering.

The maid, Ellie, was as good as her word. She not only brought the tray with a fine china cup filled with the most warming drink that Flora had ever tasted before. Along with it was a plate with a few cakes and pastries arranged on it. Flora ate with relish, she had not realised how hungry she was.

The maid placed Flora's aching feet in a bowl of warm water with a sweet smelling oil added to it. Then she set about turning her from a village girl into a lady fit to sit at the table with a real 'Sir'. Fortunately, she thought, she already knew her manners and was not coarse by nature.

Flora was embarrassed though by her obviously humble clothes, also the personal nature of the grooming which she had been put through was definitely a new experience to her, but by the time the maid was through with her, she felt much better. Ellie walked her over to a full-length looking glass and Flora gasped as she hardly recognised the young woman who looked back at her.

'Oh, Ellie, you are a treasure. I look nothing like me!' Flora took hold of the maid's hand and thanked her as if she had rescued her, as much as James had from the snow.

Ellie laughed. 'Miss, you don't look like anyone else, and nor should you. You are pretty, and now you are clean too. I don't know where you've come from or what you're doin' here, but you best remember that you are a guest of gentry. You are above the servants and you are not one of us. I won't say ought, miss, but some of the old 'uns will eat you up if you don't keep 'em in their rightful place. Do you understand what I'm sayin'?' Ellie looked at her as she bundled up Flora's discarded clothes.

'You could get into a deal of trouble yourself for talking to a guest like that couldn't you?' Flora tilted her head on one side and looked at her impishly.

'Aye, miss . . . I'd lose me job.' Ellie stopped stock-still and stared at her.

The colour seemed to drain from her face and Flora realised her small tease had scared her.

'Then it's just as well that we are to be friends, isn't it?' Flora said, and winked at her.

'Miss, you scared me half to death.' Ellie was visibly relieved; it had been a genuine fearful reaction. 'My ma is ill, you see. If I don't work I don't know what'll become of us. Pa died in the war and the lads are still away.'

'What will you do with my things?' Flora asked, changing the subject. She knew the scenario only too well.

'Have them laundered, miss.' Ellie looked at her and shook her head as if she should have known what to expect.

'Whose clothes am I wearing?' Flora asked, as she admired her reflection in the mirror once more. The neckline was lower than any she had worn before and that made her feel slightly self-conscious. Her newly washed and arranged hair, also an unusual sight, was as fine in appearance as the dress itself.

'Mr Timothy's sister left them here. When she married she had all new clothes bought for her, so her old things were just abandoned here.' Ellie shrugged as if to say it was all right for some.

'These are old?' Flora asked in disbelief.

'So it's said, but they'd be better described as having being used for a season. You rest and I'll fetch you in about an hour for dinner, miss.' She smiled at her. 'Miss, if you'll take some well-meant advice, keep your shoulders back, your chin held high and your posture straight. Look confident even if you don't feel it. You are naturally beautiful, let that knowledge be enough to take you forward in their world.'

Flora was amazed. She had never thought of herself as anything more than average in her appearance, but then she had never been preened like a peacock before.

There was one small pastry left on

the tray. 'Ellie, you have that.'

The maid looked at her and ate the fancy, licking her fingers. 'I'll come back for the tray once I've taken these down. Thank you, miss.'

Flora nodded to her and the maid left her alone.

Ellie scuttled along the hall to the servants' stairs as James was walking along the landing. He saw the clothes bundled in her arms and stopped.

'Take those to Brown and see he burns them.'

Ellie dipped a curtsey. 'Yes, Sir.' She hesitated for a moment. 'Even the boots, Sir?' she asked nervously.

'Especially the boots, Ellie!' He took a step forward. There was something in the girl's eyes, an expression of hope, that made him think again. 'Ellie, if you can put them to use then please do, but I do not wish them returned to Miss Merryman again.' The girl nodded gratefully as he continued along the landing towards Flora's door. Ellie descended by the servants' staircase.

Flora did not know what to do with herself. She was tempted to lie down and sleep, but if she did her hair would be a mess and that would be no good whatsoever. Besides, she was so excited by everything around her.

A mixture of both guilt and disbelief filled her. Everything in that room was worth more than a whole month's wage for her family — most things would keep them in food for a year, yet these objects all belonged to one family. They were so beautiful, from the inlaid ivory in the silver brushes to the marquetry on the bedside table and the hand painted silk screen.

Even the bowls on the table top were pure crystal engraved with peacocks. She was holding one in her hand and admiring the detail of the craftsmanship when there was a knock on her door. She jumped and it slipped between her fingers, she let out a cry as she reached to catch it. Fortunately, it landed on the bed and she was able to save it from falling to the floor.

'Yes, who is there?' she answered nervously, as she anxiously replaced the valuable object to its normal place. Her hands were shaking at the thought that she had nearly smashed it to smithereens.

'It is James. May I speak with you?' his voice was lowered, not as confident as he had been when they were outside in the barn.

'What, here? In the bedchamber?' she asked apprehensively.

'Yes, just for a moment.' His voice was very quiet.

Flora opened the door and saw that he too had changed and bathed. His trousers and high boots accentuated his muscular thighs and trim waist whereas his waistcoat and fitted coat contoured his broad shoulders and torso.

Flora stared at him. In turn, his eyes wandered over every aspect of her. He heard a servant on their stairs and without hesitation slid inside the room and shut the door behind him, turning the key. He took Flora by the hand and seated her next to him on the chaise-longue.

'You are indeed beautiful, Flora.' He flicked one of her carefully arranged curls with his finger, completely distracted from whatever it was that had brought him to her.

'Are we to have our chat here and now?' Flora straightened her fine skirt.

'I shall have your dinner sent up to you. I am awaiting my brother who has apparently been abed for two days suffering from some bad humours. I am about to rouse him and I do not wish you to be present when I do.

'If you hear raised voices, ignore them Flora, all will be well I promise you. The sky has cleared and I believe that soon we shall be able to travel freely once more.

'I will have to return to Frederick as soon as the road is passable, and I will send word to the militia about the murder of Reverend Eccleston.

'You know who he is . . . was?' Flora asked.

'Yes, I did. He wrote to me about the events here. Events you should never have been caught up in.' He stroked her cheek gently with his hand. She leaned into his rough palm instinctively but then remembered herself and sat upright again.

'The clothes in that cupboard are now yours. I paid for them and I give them willingly to you for I believe my cousin used you ill. He selfishly placed you in a vulnerable position knowing that the information he was gleaning from you would advance his career. He had not bargained on being sent to face Napoleon's army.' James placed her hand in his.

'You said he would come back for me. Was that a lie also?' Flora looked into his eyes. They seemed to be locked in a timeless gaze.

'Flora, he would have come back for you, rescued you from the villagers, wooed you as he already had, but your moral fibre was greater than he expected from a girl of your rank and so you were a challenge to him.'

He stopped and took a deep breath. 'I have said enough. I had not intended to be so blunt.'

'Be blunt, I need to know and you are honour bound to tell me.'

'Flora, he may have even carried out a false marriage to placate you — elopement appealed to his artistic nature; he had attempted it once before, years ago. Then he would pay your way to keep you out of his life whilst he pursued his career once more, which would inevitably include a marriage of convenience.'

James watched her closely. 'I believe you are worth a deal more than that. I must admit when I arrived on the coach I thought I was here to pick up one of Martin's usual women, fallen and quite ignorant, but you surprised me.'

Flora's eyes widened. How arrogant the man could be without even realising it. 'You describe him as if he is . . . was an opportunist, a spineless cheat, or even a coward. Is that how you wou describe your own cousin, James?' Flora saw him ponder over her words.

'He is my half-brother's cousin. Timothy is a Fforbes-Simkin. We have different mothers. Martin was the son of Timothy's mother's brother,' James explained.

'So you are saying that there is 'bad-blood'? Is yours so much better?' Flora asked indignantly.

'No . . . well, yes, in a way. There are certain traits of character that they share.' James shifted uneasily on the seat. 'Look, Flora. You are to stay here, in this room until I have sorted out various issues with Timothy and then I shall give you further instructions as to what to do before I go and fetch Frederick and inform the militia. None of this is your affair, and I am certain that you are best keeping well out of the way.' He kissed her hand and stood up. 'Admire your new garments and the time will soon pass.'

Flora stood up abruptly. 'You are suming one thing too many, James!'

122

'What is that? That you have not learned yet how to do as I ask?' He stared firmly at her and Flora realised he was quite capable of locking her in the bedchamber if she defied his instructions this time, and deemed it was for her own good.

'No, not that. I know you are only wishing to protect me. However, I did not tell anything of great import to Martin. There is nothing I have said to him that could have led him to a smuggling gang. The knowledge of them and their activities is beyond me! I merely mixed the herbs and tea and bagged or bottled up goods. So did everyone in the village. Would you have them all thrown in gaol?'

'Tell me, how did you meet him when he was staying at the Spile Inn above the village on the moor road?' James folded his arms in front of him.

'I regularly delivered supplies to them: fresh bread, pies and cake-loafs,' Flora explained, pleased with herself as she did not frequent the inn as he may have presumed originally.

'What did you take back in payment for these goods and to who?' his questions continued purposefully.

'I would take payment back,' Flora answered honestly, but then started to feel quite uneasy. Had she unwittingly been used as a go between?

'Coins?' he asked.

'Sometimes, at other times there would be a small parcel with special orders in for the soldiers' own rations.' Flora thought about the days she gave these orders to Ivy. The woman always counted her coin as soon as it was taken back but the small parcels she never opened but tucked them into her skirt's pocket.

Flora looked down at her white pumps. She had been the carrier of papers. Her own life would have been forfeit if she had been stopped and their contents disclosed. How could her friend have done that to her?

'So who is it that used you so ill, as a naïve go-between? The baker, your friend, Ivy? Who also has a relative at Ebton — Sally Riggs as was, who is now married I believe. Who was she sending you to with this.' He held up a small parcel of papers. Flora recognised it straight away. They were letters for Sally that Ivy had said she had not been able to deliver to her.

'You went through my bag?' Flora said, knowing how close she had come to losing her own liberty, if this man had not realised that she'd no part in it.

'Yes, I searched your bag when you slept, but I was sure you had no idea what information you were carrying. If you remember you let me open it and retrieve the food. I hardly think you would have done that if you knew you had confidential trade information for the French on you.'

Flora stared almost disbelievingly. She could have so easily been ruined by her only trusted friend.

'Your baker-woman I believe, wished you no ill, Flora, but having lost Martin's services and with Seth

Grieves' suspicions raised, she needed to use you one last time. This time she tried to involve me, as the perfect cover.

'When, I too, innocently wrote to her with some money for your future when Martin told me what he had promised you, she tried to dupe me, so that the espionage that she was involved in carried on under my very own protection. Your friend, Ivy, is one of the missing links in a long chain that has spanned beyond our own shores. Now, do not worry, Flora. Please stay here and do as I have asked . . . '

'Told!' she interrupted him, her heart felt as though it had been hurt yet again, not by Martin's intent, but by the betrayal of her friendship by her dear Ivy and the trouble that the woman would now be in.

'I'm asking you, Flora, to think of your own safety foremost. We shall have plenty of time together once this is over. If that is what you would wish?' He side-glanced at her a little nervously and Flora was touched as he was trying to tell her it was what he wished.

She smiled at him and nodded. 'You are still limping. How are you going to ride across treacherous roads safely on your own, James?'

He bent down and kissed her cheek lightly then unlocked the door. 'I have ridden through worse.'

'You said that you wanted my help in all this. How am I to help you if I am to stay in a bedchamber?' Flora asked.

'I will need you to complete the journey and deliver your notes to Sally, once I have cleared a few things up. If you will do that for me?'

Flora nodded. 'Just let me know when, but I hardly think my pumps will keep out the snow.' She smiled.

'Look in the long cupboard. There are at least three riding outfits. I shall come for you when the time is right. Until then stay here and be safe.' He smiled at her then left, leaving the door unlocked.

10

Flora listened as James banged his fist on the door of a room further down the hallway. It was obvious by his calls that it must be the bedchamber of his half-brother, Timothy Fforbes-Simkin.

The door was forced wide-open. 'Damnation man! How low can you stoop?' James' words echoed along the hall. Flora opened the door slightly and saw Giles rushing, as fast as he was able, along the corridor to the same bedchamber.

'How long has he been like this, Giles?' James' voice boomed from inside the room.

'Sir, he has bouts of . . . melancholy, ever since he heard of Mr Martin's and your own deaths,' Giles explained.

Flora had slipped out of her room and was listening intently. 'Sometimes he can be locked away deep in his own private world for days. I had hoped the news of your return would jolt him out of it sooner.' Giles was shaking his head to stress the hopelessness of his master's situation.

'Melancholy! Is that what you call it? Get rid of the potions.' There was a pause, 'What drug is this? Hell man, he'll kill himself through his own stupid indifference and weakness. Tell Cook to make up something to purge him. Then bring strong sweet tea and send Ellie with bowls, cloths and hot water. Tell Brown to leave the horses and his muscle will be needed here instead. We will sober the gutless wretch up, whether he wants to see the real world again or not.' James sounded utterly disgusted.

Flora heard his footsteps and returned quickly behind her door.

'He will stay a prisoner in the room until he has dried out and can eat a decent meal once more. Tell Brown he is to be with him night and day and on no account let anyone in or out of the room.'

'Yes, Sir! Straight away, Sir!' Giles turned to go back down the stairs.

'And Giles, you will then show me where the stuff is hidden.' James appeared in the hallway.

'Stuff, Sir?' Giles repeated looking up at his master with a questioning expression.

'Do you wish to keep your job here, Giles?' James' voice sounded different . . . more like the Major and less like the man she had come to know.

'Yes, Sir . . . I'll show you. I shall fetch Brown, firstly.' Giles disappeared down the stairs. James returned to Timothy but Flora saw Giles glance back over his shoulder.

Flora was peering through the gap between the door and the frame. She thought the look in his eyes was much different to the emotionally charged welcome he had given James when they had first arrived at the manor. Something in his manner made Flora feel uneasy. She ran over to the cupboard and was amazed at what she saw on opening up the painted door.

The array of gowns that were hung behind it made her stare in wonderment. Had he really meant it when he said they were now all hers? Wherever would she keep them? They would fill a cottage and she did not have one to call home. Still, her own future was a problem that was far from her mind just now.

She rummaged through the gowns and eventually found what she was looking for: a riding outfit and a pair of good quality boots. They were slightly roomy so she slipped on an extra pair of warm fine-woollen stockings and changed herself into it as soon as she could.

Once Flora was dressed she returned to the door. She was just about to open it when Ellie knocked and entered the room.

'Miss, I've brought your dinner up and . . . ' Ellie looked at Flora in amazement. 'You've changed? Surely, miss, you don't mean to go riding now?'

'Shh! Ellie. I wanted to . . . to . . . try on some new outfits. You won't tell on me, will you?' Flora looked at the girl with an impish smile.

'No, just take care not to get caught.' She put down the tray. 'Do you wish me to come back when I've done my chores and help you put them back?'

The girl looked tired. Flora smiled broadly at her. 'No, Ellie. I'll leave the tray outside the room when I've finished and then I'll lock the door. You can come in the morning.' Flora sat down to eat her food. She was hungry and it smelt delicious.

'Thank you, miss, I'll make sure you're not to be disturbed.' Ellie looked well-pleased as she left.

Flora ate quickly. It was just too good to leave. Once finished, she placed the tray outside the door and closed it again quickly.

Moments later James left Timothy's bedchamber. He paused as he saw the tray outside her door and closed it again quickly.

Flora had closed the door too, her heartbeat quickened as she waited to hear him run down the stairs. He was thinking of coming to her, she knew it, but she could not open the door to him dressed as she was or he would lock her in for her own safety.

He must have thought better of it as he continued down the stairs. Flora heard his voice raised downstairs. She ran to the long window at the end of her room. It overlooked the side of the house and she could just see the end of the stable block.

A horse had been brought out and was being made ready. The snow was softening and no more had fallen all day. Still treacherous, Flora thought, but she was sure the thaw had set in.

Flora was expecting James to mount the animal, but was surprised when it was a man from the stable who climbed into the saddle. Then she realised what had been staring her in the face. The animal was James' own horse. 'However did it get here?' she said to herself, as she stepped back, watching the rider leave.

She knew that she had to warn James, but was at a disadvantage as she did not know the layout of the house. Undaunted, Flora was determined to be of help. She tiptoed out of her room, locking the door behind her and dropped the key inside her pocket. Slowly, she made her way along the dark hallway.

She could hear a voice from Timothy's bedchamber. 'Here, man, you drink this, milord. Let Brown worry about that troublesome brother of yours.' His voice was low but it was obvious that far from purging the man, he was giving him more liquor. They were blatantly disobeying James' orders which meant only one thing — he was in great danger.

Flora was about to step on to the top step of the main stairs when a hand grabbed her arm and pulled her back.

She turned quickly; the thought that the manservant, Brown, had discovered her made her gasp but it was the maid, Ellie, who put a finger to her lips and led her down the servants' stairs. As they reached the bare stone passage at the bottom Ellie turned quickly away from what appeared by the noise and smells to be the kitchen passage, instead leading her to a room full of damp wet linen, suspended on large wooden frames from the ceiling. This was obviously part of the laundry rooms.

'What do yer think you are doin, miss?' Ellie whispered but her desperate tone raised the pitch of the girl's voice. 'And don't give me any of the nonsense that yer told me in that room up there. Do yer think I was born yesterday?' She stared Flora straight in the eye.

'Can I trust you, Ellie?' Flora asked, realising it was a ridiculous question.

'Well, if yer can't, I wouldn't like to be in your shoes just now!' Ellie was vexed with her. 'You were told to stay put, weren't you?'

'Brown, and I think Giles, are

plotting against him. They are up to something.' Flora held the girl's arm almost imploringly.

'Please, miss, you are becoming involved in things you don't under-stand . . . '

'I know exactly what I am involved in and I want to save James from them. He is a good man,' Flora said defen-sively.

'I saw him go to the stable after Benjamin was set out. Look, I'll be missed soon. I'll take Cook's attention, you go out that door over there and cross the yard; mind it's slippery as hell underfoot.'

Flora nodded, 'Thank you . . . '

'Don't thank me, miss. If you are caught I can do no more to help you. I have me ma to consider. They'd take us both to market, without a thought for her.'

Flora nodded again. She understood and the thought that she too would have become a commodity to be sold at auction — lost and abandoned filled her with fear as she realised how serious the situation had become. When Flora heard the girl chattering away to someone in the kitchens, Flora slipped outside. The clothes she was wearing were far warmer and more suitable to her old ones.

11

Flora could see her own breath as she crept along the outside of the manor, keeping to the shadows, until she dared to make a run across the melting snow. Once inside she saw James saddling a horse himself. He was just about to lead the animal out when the voice of Giles warned him, 'Sir, be sure to take the low road. The salt air from the sea winds stopped the snow lying so deep. It will be all but clear by now, I should think; although this weather tis treacherous enough, Sir.'

'Thank you for your advice, Giles. I shall be back before morning. See that my brother is well on his way to being coherent by the time I return.' James walked out of the stables leading the horse, Giles walking at his side. Flora was hidden in the shadows behind the end stall, hardly daring to breathe.

She wanted to shout out, but to do so would be folly. So she waited. Flora heard James kick the horse on, and as she peered saw Giles return into the warmth of the manor.

Flora looked at the only animal left in the stable; it was a work-horse like the one that she had often helped Seth hitch up to his cart as a girl. It took some moments but she eventually found enough pieces of sack-cloth and twine to cover the beast's hooves. Then with reins and a saddle in place she walked it carefully out. Silently as she could, she raised herself into the saddle.

'Here!' Ellie's whisper nearly caused her to bolt the horse straight into a gallop. The girl had tiptoed across the yard handing her a leather pouch. 'A pistol, take care, miss.'

She ran back inside and Flora placed it in her pocket then kicked the animal onwards. Ellie had helped her further despite her fear of retribution. Her mount had an ungainly amble more than a stride. The wrappings soon came off the animal's hooves which Flora decided was just as well as it saved her from dismounting before reaching the road. She followed the tracks of James' mount and turned right outside the estate walls. Excitement and fear appeared to race around her equally.

She had not travelled more than a few hundred yards when a mounted figure pulled out of the woods, a pistol pointed at her head.

Highwayman! Flora thought to herself and considered trying to make her escape, but she was hardly riding an Arabian racehorse. She cursed her rotten luck and felt for the pistol within her pocket; not that she knew if it were loaded or how to use it.

'Keep still, woman, or I'll blast your head from your shoulders.' The voice was educated, but not that of James.

'If it is money you want I have none on me.' Flora strained to see who had stopped her, but she could not in the poor light.

'No, I do not wish your money.' The

voice had changed slightly, it was not so deep as the original call that he had made. There was something familiar about it, and then realisation dawned.

'It is Frederick, isn't it?' she asked excitedly.

He lowered the pistol and placed it back in his holster. 'Yes, miss, it is, and you have no business being out here this night.' He moved alongside her.

'James is in danger, Frederick, a man has already been sent out to lay in wait for him. We might already be too late!' Flora moved off.

'He was told to take the low road.' Flora added this vital information as they continued at speed along the wintry track.

A few miles along, Frederick peeled off the road on to a woodland track. 'Where are you taking me, Frederick?' Flora was a little nervous; surely Frederick was to be trusted? If not, then she wondered if she would ever trust another soul again. She thought fleetingly of Ivy, but that was too painful a betrayal for her, so she concentrated on the way ahead. There was no other direction for her to go in any sense of the word.

Stopping in a clearing where the road was visible below them, Frederick looked at her. 'Because, miss, that was my instruction, to meet here and, unlike you, I know how to obey my betters.'

Flora was incensed by his arrogant smile. She was about to turn her cumbersome beast round when James' voice spoke out.

'Will you never do as I say, woman?' He was standing on a fallen tree trunk on a bank to her right.

'James! You are in great danger. A man was sent out on horse before you left and Brown and Giles are both in some kind of league. They keep your brother in the stupor and . . . ' She hesitated, seeing the familiar look of humour on James' face. He was standing there, somewhat relaxed in manner. 'You knew. You realised all along, yet you left me there, why?' She stared up at him and he jumped down and walked to her side.

'For your own good, and so as not to raise their suspicion. If you had only done as I asked you would have been quite safe, Flora. Tomorrow morning the militia will arrive after they have made arrests within the region. Frederick, here, managed to continue to Newcastle, where he delivered certain papers to the Customs office there. He is a trusted friend, and my ward.' Frederick dipped his head at her as if he had just been formerly introduced.

'Why did you not stay yourself then?' Flora looked down at James' face. He looked both tired and troubled.

'Because I had no way of knowing for sure that Frederick had managed to get through. Then there is this Riggs woman, or, more accurately, her husband who is well-known along this shore but difficult to catch in the act. If the militia march into the seaside town they will all go to ground, all evidence hidden in many a curious way, so I was going to try and deliver the papers myself, trying to keep you away from them, and safe.'

'Well, I am here now. So let me help you as I came here to do. Give me the papers, I shall ride in on this old workhorse, and in the morrow, I will tell you whatever you need to know. I am expected, and my delay can be put down to the weather. Did you find the man who went out before you?' Flora saw a smile across his face.

'He will not be bothering anyone again.' He produced the letters from an inside pocket and placed them inside her own. He retrieved the pouch with the pistol inside it, and looked at her with a worried expression.

'Do you know how to use this?' he asked.

'No, Ellie gave me it. She's a good girl,' Flora explained how the maid had tried to help her.

'She is Frederick's sister, which is why he foolishly lied about his age and tried to join the army in order that his mother and sister would be better provided for, only like many a gullible youth, he was told lies and nearly lost his liberty and life. They will be well taken care of when all this is done.

'Now, you must carry on down this road, into the village. Ask for the house of Sally Riggs and follow what instructions Ivy gave you regarding your welcome message. Say nothing of me, only that I left you with Frederick and the coachman, and you paid for the nag from the inn as soon as the weather eased. Now, give me your hat and step down.'

'Why?' Flora asked, as she climbed down, his arms receiving her as she slid effortlessly into them.

He looked at her and she felt the same urge as him, but both were aware that young eyes looked on.

Frederick discreetly turned his back to them and stared aimlessly at the road beneath the woods.

James' lips found hers, his arms

brought her nearer to him and he kissed her with a feeling of love and passion that consumed her whole being. It was after some moments and with some reluctance that they parted.

He tossed her hat into the woods. 'Why ever did you do that?' she asked as the expensive hat was discarded.

'Because, my dear Flora, you look like you have been in a ladies' costumiers. We need to rough you up a little. He removed pins from her hair until it hung loose about her shoulders. Then it was tied in a simpler manner. Her boots were scuffed, although it grieved her to have to do it and her clothes dirtied. They were a size too large, which added to the overall appearance that they had not been made for her and had been cast off.

'For once in my life I really felt special, now look at me!' Flora said, disgusted at what had happened to her appearance.

'You are very special and shall look it again. You shall return to poverty for only a short time, I promise. But I shall keep the pistol. It is dangerous, particularly in the hands of one who has never used one before. Now, go, my love and take great care. You will see me the morrow.'

He helped her to remount and she made her way back down the track to the road, following it down to the fishing village of Ebton, nervous at what adventure was to come, but warmed throughout as he had called her 'his love', and after his kiss she realised that whatever fondness she had felt towards Martin, it had been girlish foolery. For James she would risk her life and he for her. That indeed was true love.

12

Flora rode the large cumbersome horse down the track that descended steeply to sea level. Before her lay a sweeping sandy bay, framed between two headlands. She could see an inn at the bottom of the under cliff, and what looked to her to be a blacksmiths-cum-store behind it. A boatmaker's shed surrounded by crab pots and nets was at the other side, then a line of about a dozen higgledy-piggledy cottages almost on the flat sandy beach itself.

She stopped for a moment. There was something beautiful about the simplicity of the place set against such a dramatic back-drop, but it was rough and rugged like, she thought, the people themselves. The cobbles were lined upon the beach. She passed the inn and walked the horse onward as there was no noise from inside, but she thought she saw a candle flicker in the small window. Outside the black-smiths she saw a man wearing a leather apron lifting a broken wheel. He no doubt doubled as the wheelwright, she thought.

'Excuse me, sir.' She approached him carefully; he was large of frame and strong. The beard on his face made him look older than perhaps he was. 'Could you tell me where Sally Riggs lives?'

He let the wheel drop with a bang upon his bench and picked up a heavy hammer. 'Can't tell anyone where Sally Riggs lives.' His voice was gruff. He hammered a broken piece of metal. It fell heavily to the ground. 'Who wants to know?'

Although he seemed to be absorbed with the wheel, he was watching her closely.

'I am a friend of hers who has been sent to her by her relative, Ivy Dunton, from over the moor.'

He looked at her and stepped around the bench. She was still on the old horse, but doubted she would be able to race it back up the steep track if she needed to escape quickly. The beach would be the best route, she thought to herself, or the wooded gill behind the inn. None of them appeared to hold much hope for her.

'Ivy won't have heard the news yet then.' He came over to her and stroked the horse's nose, calming it down.

'Heard what?' Flora asked. She did not trust this man and she felt very alone in this desolate place.

'Sally doesn't 'live' anywhere anymore. She died, miss, giving birth to a boy child. He died shortly afterwards, so if yer looking for a home her husband, Benjamin, has room in his cottage. You'll find him in there.' He pointed to the inn.

'I don't want to disturb him in his grief. I'll go and tell Ivy the sad news and return her letters to her. She, like myself, will be most upset by this sad day's news. Good day, sir.' Flora tried to move the horse away, but he held the animal firmly by the bridle.

'Now, lass, you only just arrived here, so don't go runnin' off.' He held the horse with a hand either side of its head. Flora realised she was going nowhere. 'Benjamin!' he bellowed at the top of his voice. She flinched. 'Now you just climb down here as I'm sure Benjamin will want to speak to such a pretty young friend of Sally's as you.'

Flora hesitated, but then a voice from behind her answered the man's call. 'So, Flora, you finally arrived. I've been expectin' yer, but not on an old nag. Get down and take a drink with me.'

Flora looked at the small inn.

'Not in there; that's a heathen place if ever there was, lass. No, in my own home whilst Samuel looks after the beast.'

He was a stocky man but seemed friendly enough so Flora dismounted, knowing she had little choice in the matter anyway. When she turned around a group of about ten people had appeared from various cottage doorways.

13

The man, Benjamin, cupped her arm and walked her along the row to the end cottage. 'I thought yer would have a bag or somethin' with you not an old nag.' He looked down at her, and she could see that he was in his middle years. His eyes were as bright as buttons despite the fact he had been drinking and smelled heavily of ale.

'I sold my things at the inn to pay for the 'nag'. There was no other way of getting through here. The coach could go no further and the driver was worried about the mail being late.'

'Aye, he'd care more about that than his own passengers.'

Flora thought she sounded plausible and he seemed to believe her.

'Well I dare say you could use some of Sally's things. She won't need 'em no more. So you have come at a good time. I need a good woman around here and you need a home, so Ivy sent word. Looks like we can make a good match.' He winked at her.

Flora glanced at him and saw that he was smiling, showing a gap where teeth were missing. She hoped he was joking, but there was a note of hope within his jest that made her long for James' arms around her once more.

'So give me the letters and I'll see that young Samuel sends word back that you arrived safely.' He opened the old wooden door to the small cruck-built cottage. It had a stone-flagged floor which had a fine covering of sand upon it. Flora thought it must be a full-time job keeping it swept clean.

There was a small fire at one end, a table in the middle with two chairs by it and a bed at the other. A narrow ladder led to an open room below the thatch that looked like it was being used as a storage area. Flora thought of James' fine home, light with its flickering oil lamps and compared it to this poky little hovel where a tallow candle created a dim ineffective light and smelled foul.

'The letters, lass.' He put his hand out.

She reached into her pocket and produced the small packet that Ivy had given her.

He took them from her and smiled. 'You make yersel' a drink, I'll be back in a moment then we can talk about what I'd be expectin' of yer.'

Benjamin left her. She stood peering out of the doorway and watched him return to the inn and the man Samuel. Flora saw something move and realised that an old hag was watching her from the adjacent cottage. She closed the door and looked at the window on the opposite side of the room. It overlooked the beach.

Flora opened it as wide as she could and thought that if she breathed in she might just be able to squeeze through the gap. It was tight and she tore her sorely abused new outfit but she managed to lower herself on to the beach.

As the cottage was at the end of the row, she ran along the beach hidden from the others by the dunes. Not wanting to be easily tracked and followed she headed up into the coarse marram grass.

It was hard running on such fine sand as it gave way beneath her boots until she managed to get on to the grass-covered dunes.

She heard a horse's hooves at the gallop and stared around her from her lowered position. The man Samuel was riding on a strong mount up the bank. He must be taking the letters on to their contact. What was she to do now? With no Sally here, she had a man of low morals on her tail. He was obviously not grieving for his wife.

She felt so sad as the girl had been so full of life and fun and to think of her ending her days in such a way, in such a place, sickened Flora. It was not going to happen to her, of that she was sure.

14

A shot rang out and she dropped to the ground. Flora's heart beat faster. She ran almost on all fours until she could get over the largest dune and away from the village, but then worse still she found she was in a low-lying marshland. Flora did not stop to look back to see who was shooting. She presumed it had been a warning shot to her to stop. But, to her surprise, the shot was returned and the solitary shots became a volley.

Then the sound of sword hitting sword was heard and Flora realised that there was a fight — a small battle taking place on the beach. She crawled up to the top of the dune and could just see a Revenue cutter had landed men by the headland. They had sneaked around the bay and were engaged in a fight with the village men and women.

Flora stood up and was about to descend the sandy bank.

'I called you a harlot and a wanton woman. I turned your own folk against you, Flora Merryman.'

Flora spun around and lost her footing. She fell and rolled down the bank, her riding skirt wrapping itself around her legs as sand stuck to her face and hair.

'Seth!' she spat the word out with the gritty sand. She struggled to stand by which time Seth was standing in front of her, his pistol still in his hand.

'I did it for good reason, Flora.' He offered her a hand and she pulled herself upright. She stared straight into the old familiar face, who she had respected and feared as a child. 'I don't mind the trade, Flora, but I'll stand no truck with traitors, whether they be Ivy Duncan or you or both. So I'll not ask your forgiveness, lass, but I'll take yer back to yer fancy man and he can take yer to where you'll be safe.'

'Martin, never was 'my fancy man'

and he is dead anyway,' she answered defiantly. However, inside she felt greatly relieved as she thought she was about to be blown to kingdom come by the man.

'I didn't mean him.' He walked her by a path through the marsh that she would never have found on her own, saying no more until they approached two men on horseback.

James smiled down at her. 'You really are a sight,' he said unsympathetically and dismounted. 'For sore eyes,' he added as he held out a hand to her. 'Thank you, Seth. You have done well.'

Seth nodded. 'I don't hold with traitors, but she best not be seen in our village again, Sir, if you know what's good for her.'

The man turned and walked off into the marsh as if he were on a solid path. No wonder, she thought, they have been so hard to track down.

'Do I know what's good for you, Flora?' he asked as he brushed the sand from her hair.

'I think so,' she whispered as he kissed her lips, and Frederick turned discreetly away from them, looking out over a desolate marshland, whilst James and Flora embraced each other and secured their future.

We do hope that you have enjoyed reading this large print book.

Did you know that all of our titles are available for purchase?

We publish a wide range of high quality large print books including:
Romances, Mysteries, Classics
General Fiction
Non Fiction and Westerns

Special interest titles available in large print are:
The Little Oxford Dictionary
Music Book, Song Book
Hymn Book, Service Book

Also available from us courtesy of Oxford University Press:
Young Readers' Dictionary
(large print edition)
Young Readers' Thesaurus
(large print edition)

For further information or a free brochure, please contact us at:
Ulverscroft Large Print Books Ltd.,
The Green, Bradgate Road, Anstey,
Leicester, LE7 7FU, England.
Tel: (00 44) **0116 236 4325**
Fax: (00 44) **0116 234 0205**

Other titles in the
Linford Romance Library:

NEVER LET ME GO

Toni Anders

It was love at first sight for Nurse Chloe Perle and ambitious Dr. Adam Raven, but their employer had plans for his daughter, Susannah, and the young doctor. When Adam informed Chloe his career would always come before romantic entanglements, she left the practice for a position far away in the Cotswolds. There, she attracted the attention of Benedict, a handsome young artist. Afraid that he had lost Chloe forever, Adam begged her friend, Betty, the only person who knew her whereabouts, to help him.